GUINEA DOG 2

Other Books by Patrick Jennings

Guinea Dog

Lucky Cap

Invasion of the Dognappers

My Homework Ate My Homework

Guinea Dog 2

Patrick Jennings

EGMONT
USA
NEW YORK

EGMONT

We bring stories to life

First published by Egmont USA, 2013
443 Park Avenue South, Suite 806
New York, NY 10016

1 3 5 7 9 8 6 4 2

www.egmontusa.com
www.patrickjennings.com

Library of Congress Cataloging-in-Publication Data

Jennings, Patrick.
Guinea dog 2 / Patrick Jennings.
p. cm
Summary: The laughs continue when Fido, the guinea pig that thinks she's a dog, has a pup that behaves strangely, too. A sequel to Guinea Dog—
ISBN 978-1-60684-452-6 (hardback) — ISBN 978-1-60684-453-3 (ebook)
[1. Guinea pigs—Fiction. 2. Family life—Fiction. 3. Schools—Fiction.]
I. Title. II. Title: Guinea dog two.
PZ7.J4298715Guf 2013
[Fic]—dc23
2013000979

Printed in the United States of America

For the stupendous
Ro Stimo

Contents

1. I wanted a dog.

I got a guinea pig instead. At first I was devastated. How could my mom think a guinea pig could replace a dog? I knew she was just trying to be nice, but still . . .

Mom knew I was crushed that my dad wouldn't let me have a dog. The guy doesn't like dogs. Is that nuts or what? He has a long list of reasons why he'll never let me have one. I have a long list of reasons why I want one. But his reasons always win. Why? Because he's the dad. He works at home. He gets to make the call. He's the umpire, and the dog is always out.

So Mom brought home a guinea pig, and guess what? Dad didn't like it, either. What does the guy like? Quiet. Order. Perfect grammar.

The guy's as much fun as a standardized test.

He insisted we bring "the infernal creature" back to the pet shop, but when we did, Petopia wasn't there anymore. In one day, it had closed up and disappeared for good.

So instead of a dog I got stuck with a guinea pig. I named her Fido, the name I'd been saving for the dog I'd been wanting all my life and, tragically, would never get.

But as it turned out, Fido is no ordinary guinea pig. She does a lot of strange things.

- She growls.
- She howls.
- She whines.
- She pants.
- She barks.
- She yaps when someone is at the door.
- She snarls at the mail carrier.
- She bites the mail carrier.
- She obeys commands. She sits, heels, speaks, and rolls over when I tell her to.

- She licks herself.
- She licks my face.
- She licks my face after she licks herself.
- She eats dog food.
- She begs for table food.
- She eats meat.
- She eats cheese.
- She eats pie.
- She eats poop.
- She eats dead things.
- Her breath smells like meat, cheese, pie, dead things, and poop.
- She runs up to me when I come home from school.
- She chews up my homework.
- She chews up Dad's shoes.
- She chews bones.
- She buries bones.
- She buries Dad's shoes.
- She sleeps at the foot of my bed.
- She dreams she's running. Her little paws wave in the air.
- She snores.
- She walks on a leash.

- She wears a collar with tags. (A cat collar, actually, but she doesn't know that.)
- She marks her territory.
- She runs alongside my bike.
- She chases cats and squirrels.
- She plays with dogs.
- She sniffs them.
- She gets in fights.
- She gets fleas.
- She plays Fetch.
- She plays Tug-of-War.
- She catches Frisbees.
- She sleeps inside a little doghouse with her name painted on it.
- She runs for help when I fall in a river and break my foot.
- She takes care of me when I'm laid up with a broken foot.
- She defends me from evil.
- She's loyal, steadfast, and true.
- She needs me.

In other words, she acts like a dog.

She isn't a dog, though. She's a fat orange

guinea pig with a white mohawk. My best friend, Murphy, calls her a guinea dog.

After Fido rescued me from the river and took care of me and kept me company while I got better, I stopped minding that she wasn't an actual dog. I didn't care that she was a guinea dog. She was *my* guinea dog, and I wouldn't trade her for anything.

Then my foot got better, and I was forced to go back to school.

2. My guinea dog waits at the front door, her leash in her mouth.

"Sorry, Fido," I say. "We're not going for a walk. I have to go back to school."

She whimpers and paws at my bulky black medical boot, which fits over my cast and helps me walk. I've been getting around okay using it and my crutches, so long as Fido doesn't trip me up.

"I've got her," Dad says from behind me. He kneels down and scoops her up. "We're going to be just fine today without Rufus, aren't we, Fido?" He tickles her fat orange neck. She pants.

Dad has sure changed his mind about Fido since Mom first brought her home. Somehow she won him over.

She did the same thing to me.

We climb into Dad's hybrid. Mom already left in hers to go to the hardware store, where she mixes paint for a living. Fido stood on my armrest all the way to school, her nose out the window, her mohawk fluttering in the wind.

"Be careful today on those crutches," Dad says. "You don't want to end up missing more school."

I don't?

"Roof!" Murphy calls out when we pull up in front of the school. He runs up to the car and tickles Fido under her chin. She licks his fingers. "Hey, girl! You coming to school, too?"

Fido's rear end wags like crazy. She looks back at me as if she's asking, *Can I? Can I? Please? Can I?*

"Now look how worked up she is," I say, scowling at Murph. "Don't lead her on like that."

I hand her to Dad, then open my door. It's not easy getting in and out of a car with a cast and crutches, let me tell you. It's funny how many simple things I took for granted before I broke my foot. Stairs, for example. I used to run up and down them without a second thought. Not anymore.

"Eager to get back to your education, I bet," Murph says, giving me his hand.

"I've been keeping up on my classwork," I say. "Have you?"

"Keep an eye on him, will you, Murphy?" my dad asks before Murph answers. "Remind him to stay off that foot whenever possible."

Murph smiles. He's glad Dad changed the subject. Which means he's probably not keeping up.

Murphy's one of the most likable kids in school, but not exactly one of its best students. He's practically failing. I've been trying to help him, but it's not easy getting him to take something seriously.

"You can count on me, Art," he says. Art is my dad's name. It's short for Arthur. "But I have a feeling he's going to get hoisted onto people's shoulders and carried around instead of having to walk. The guy's practically a hero at Rustbury Elementary."

"What?" I ask. "What are you talking about?"

"Everybody knows you broke your foot crossing a raging river filled with snapping turtles . . ."

Which is not what happened. Kaiser Creek is shallow and slow, and there aren't any snapping turtles.

". . . and everyone knows your trustworthy guinea dog saved you."

Murphy loves making up stories. It's one of the reasons everyone likes him. He has a way of making everything more fun. But sometimes he goes too far.

As if to prove my point, a group of kids call out my name, then rush toward us. My face feels as if it's on fire. I'm not used to getting attention. I'm used to Murphy getting it all.

My instinct is to hide. But first I need to hide Fido. No dog likes being rushed by a mob of kids. Not even a guinea dog. And judging by the crazed looks on these kids' faces, I need to get Fido to safety.

"Go!" I say to my dad and slam the door.

He drives off just as the kids reach us. More

like hit us. *Wham!* I try to stay upright, but it's impossible.

The mob bombards me with questions:

"Does your guinea pig really act like a dog?"

"Does it bark?"

"Does it bite?"

"Does it do tricks?"

"Did it really save twin babies from a burning building?"

"And stop a bank robbery?"

"And rescue a man buried by an avalanche?"

"And chase an escaped circus lion back into his cage?"

"Can I come over to your house and see it?"

"Where can I get one?"

"All right! All right!" Murphy says loudly. "Back up! Move back! Let's not break any more of the kid's bones!"

They listen to him, as always.

"*This* is being hoisted?" I yell at him from the ground. "*This* is being carried around like a hero?"

"*This,* my brave young friend," he says, pulling me up, "is the price of fame. Get used to it."

3. I pity celebrities.

Especially the ones with broken bones. Olympic athletes. Super Bowl quarterbacks. Everywhere they go, people mob them, even when they have casts and crutches. I can relate.

I've never had a harder time getting into the school building. Murphy holds my arm and guides me through the crowd, yelling at them to move away. You can tell he's enjoying himself. He's getting the attention he lives for. And I think he likes that I'm getting some, too. I don't know why. I don't like the attention, which includes being rammed by some kid and twirling around like a ballerina on the toe of my medical boot. A ballerina with crutches. Not so graceful.

Actually, that would be one of the few ballets I wouldn't mind seeing.

Thankfully, Murph catches me before the twirling results in a crash landing. I glare up at him as he holds me in his heroic arms. I am not supposed to be doing pirouettes. I'm supposed to be staying off my bad foot, and it's his need for attention that has gotten me into this stupid situation.

"Your dad asked me to remind you to stay off that foot," he says, pretending to be dead serious. "So . . . stay off it."

He turns to the crowd. "You guys've got to give this guy a break. Oh, I forgot! He already *has* one!"

The crowd laughs. I don't understand why. Puns aren't funny.

"Seriously?" I ask. "This is the time for jokes?"

He lifts my arm, tucks his head under my armpit, then stands up straight, supporting me.

"Man down!" he says. "Clear a path! I've got to get this man to safety! Step back! Man down! Step back!"

They obey him again . . . for a few seconds . . . then swoop back in for another attack. Dmitri is in front.

"I want a guinea dog, dude," he says through gritted teeth. "Get me one. I'll pay. You can name your price."

He sounds annoyed. He must be frustrated that he can't get what he wants when he wants it.

If Murph is my best friend—and today he's testing it—Dmitri is my worst. He came to my house a couple of times when I was laid up, *after* he found out about Fido. He's the kind of kid who has to have the coolest stuff in the world, so naturally, he wanted Fido for his collection. I wouldn't let him have her, of course, so he got mad and said that Fido couldn't be the only guinea dog in the world. He said she wasn't special. Which made me mad.

"Couldn't find one online, eh?" I ask.

He seethes, which is no big deal. The guy's a natural-born seether. Like a car radiator on a scorching summer day, you never know when he's going to boil over.

"No time to chat," Murph grunts at him. "Got to get this man out of harm's way."

Dmitri boils over, but Murph keeps us moving on toward the cafeteria's double doors. Students are allowed to hang out in the cafeteria before school, but usually I spend the time on the playground. Murphy never arrives before school. He's always late. So this will make a nice change for both of us.

If we ever get there. I've never wanted to sit down more in my life.

I don't like being crowded. I don't like being knocked down. What's the matter with these people anyway? Can't they see I'm on crutches?

I also don't like having so many people prying into my private life. And my pet's private life. I don't get into their faces and ask tons of questions about their pets. They act as if Fido were some sort of freak. She isn't.

Well, maybe she is.

But who isn't?

4. Speaking of freaks, here comes Lurena.

She's the weird girl in my class who dresses like an American Girl doll: long flowery dresses, belts, vests, hats with fake flowers. She was with my family and me the day I broke my foot. My mom invited her to the river, completely without my permission. When I was laid up, Lurena kept dropping by our house, uninvited, to see how I was. She usually brought along her rodent pets—her hamster and chinchilla—to play with Fido. Fido snarled and chased them under the furniture. She doesn't like rodents. Other than herself.

"Will you leave him alone?" Lurena yells. "What is the matter with you? He has a broken foot! Get away from him!"

She runs toward us, her blond curls bouncing and her face all red.

The crowd backs off a bit, like they're scared of her. Even the boys.

"Are you crazy or what?" she asks, shoving Dmitri, who rushed in when the others stepped back. "He's on *crutches*, for crying out loud!"

This is awkward. I mean, I appreciate her taking my side, but Lurena is a girl, after all.

Dmitri loves it.

"See you got a girl to fight your battles for you," he snarls.

"Battles?" I ask. "I'm just trying to get into the building without breaking another bone or two."

"And I just want a guinea dog," Dmitri shoots back.

"Well, you're out of luck," Lurena says. "Now go kick a kickball or something and leave this poor boy alone."

Dmitri and a couple of other boys snicker.

"Okay, *poor* boy," Dmitri says, stepping away backward. "We'll leave you alone, you *poor, poor* boy."

A few of the boys follow him toward the playground, pointing back at me and snickering all the way.

"Thanks so much," I say to Lurena.

"You're welcome," she says, not getting my tone. "What a bunch of lunkheads. I mean, *really*!"

"They are lunkheads," Murph pipes in. "Their heads are lunks. Great big lunks."

"What's a lunk?" I ask.

He shrugs. "Not completely sure."

"Stop fooling around, Murph, and let's get him inside," Lurena says. "What are you doing here so early anyway? You're never on time for school."

Murphy checks his wrist. He doesn't wear a watch. "Why, *I'm early*! I've got to get home!"

He lets go of me suddenly, and I start to tumble to the ground. Lurena catches me.

"Get back here!" I yell. "You got me into this, and you're going to stay by my side all day! Like a loyal, trustworthy friend!"

"Of course I am!" he says, and slaps his

forehead. "What was I thinking! You must resume your education before your brain starts going all soft and mushy!"

"Just help me, will you?" I glare at him, trying to open his eyes to the fact that Lurena is cradling me in her arms.

He pulls me up by my arm and hooks it over his shoulder. "Please, miss," he says to Lurena, "grab hold of his other arm and let's get him into the building, stat. That means at once."

"I know what stat means," Lurena says.

She takes my other arm, and my crutches drop to the ground. I lose my balance and fall backward, dragging the two of them with me. As we lie on the sidewalk with everyone standing above us, laughing uncontrollably, I spot an animal galloping across the lawn. It's small and furry, and its tongue is hanging out of its mouth. It's not a cat. It's not a dog . . . exactly. It has a mohawk. A white one.

5. I'm almost positive guinea pigs can't open car doors.

I doubt they could survive a leap out the window of a moving vehicle, either. But when it comes to Fido, anything is possible.

"Fido!" I call out, then immediately regret it. This bunch is so worked up, they might stampede her.

"It's the guinea dog!" they start yelling. "It's the guinea dog!"

Fido stops in her tracks and makes a small, scared yelp. I don't think she likes being targeted by a mob, either.

The crowd rushes toward her. She does a one-eighty and flees as fast as she can.

"Save her!" I yell at Murphy and Lurena,

who have gotten to their feet. "Save Fido!"

Lurena is first out of the gate, with Murphy right behind her. I work on getting up, which is not easy. Stupid crutches! Stupid boot! Stupid, stupid *foot*!

"Don't chase her into the street!" I scream, because that's exactly where Fido is heading. I shudder, thinking she might run in front of a school bus. "Circle around, Murph! Head her off!"

"I'm on it!" Murphy answers, and picks up speed. He's faster than Fido and should be able to get in front of her.

Unfortunately, the other kids got a head start, and some of them are pretty fast, especially Dmitri. I think he's the fastest. Probably because he wants Fido the most.

I wonder what he'll do if he catches her? Would he give her back to me?

"Lurena!" I yell. "Stop Dmitri!" I feel so powerless. A herd of kids bearing down on Fido, and I can't do anything but yell. It's awful.

Lurena flashes a thumbs-up, then turns and runs straight at Dmitri, her long dress flapping like a flag in the wind. Surprisingly, she's faster than he is. Probably because she doesn't like him, and because she really likes Fido.

When she gets close enough, she takes a dive at his knees and brings him down. Boy, is he mad, but Lurena doesn't hang around to listen to him tell her off. She bounces to her feet and races after Fido. She doesn't even brush the dried leaves and twigs out of her long hair.

Murphy heads Fido off at the row of hedges that mark the edge of school grounds. He kneels down.

"Here, girl," he says in a kind voice. He crouches and reaches out a hand. "Here, Fido. Come on. Come here, girl."

Fido streaks straight to him—and straight between his legs. Straight into the bushes. And she's gone.

Her pursuers stop their pursuit and groan. You're not allowed to leave school grounds once you're on them.

"Nice catch," I say to Murphy, as I hobble over.

"Sorry," he says. "I forgot she's so small. How'd she get away from your dad?"

"I have no idea, but she's good at getting away."

"I remember when she sneaked into your backpack," Lurena says, walking over.

"That was some tackle," Murph says. "Considered going out for the Steelers?"

"I have to find Fido."

"You can't leave school grounds. And if you find her, you can't bring her into the building. Pet rodents aren't allowed in school." She scowls. "Which is a totally unfair rule, by the way."

"I'll help you find her," Murph says. "Even if it makes me late for class."

"Gee, thanks for making the supreme sacrifice."

"I'll help, too," Lurena says.

This is surprising. Lurena is Miss Perfect Attendance. But then she's also the Rodent Queen.

"Thanks," I say, then cup my hands around my mouth and call, "Fido, come! Come, Fido!"

She pokes her head out of the hedge. She pants a few times. She runs at me. She's always been such an obedient dog. Er, pig. Er, rodent.

"Cool!" someone says.

"Did you see that?" asks someone else.

"It came when he called!"

"It really is trained!"

"Just like a dog!"

"Fifty bucks for it!" This is Dmitri.

"She's not for sale, Dmitri," Lurena says. "Get it through your thick skull."

"Still got her fighting your battles, eh, Rufus? What, are you guys married or something?"

He looks ready to boil over again.

The bell rings. Thank Dog. The crowd heads inside.

Fido trots up to me. I bend over to pet her . . . and fall on my head.

"Darn crutches!" I growl. "Darn Dad!"

You'd think an adult would be able to hold on to one fat little rodent, wouldn't you?

"Rufus!" a voice calls out.

It's Dad. Did he hear me?

He's getting out of his car, which he's parked in the street diagonally over two parking spaces. Not very Dad-like. He runs over without shutting his door. Also, not very Dad-like.

"Have you seen Fido?" he asks, out of breath. He doesn't exercise enough. Mom always tells him that.

Fido pops out from behind me. Fortunately, I didn't crush her when I fell.

"Yes," I say.

"She jumped out the window when I stopped at an intersection," Dad says, as if it's the most shockingly rude thing he'd ever seen. "I got out to catch her, and she just took off!" He stops and holds his side, like he has a cramp. "I ran after her."

"So I see."

"Well, I'll take her. You three should get inside. I heard the bell. School's starting."

"Are you sure you won't let her get away again?" I ask.

He gives me the Stony Stare.

"Okay," I say. "Fido, go to Dad."

She whimpers.

"You heard me. Go."

She hangs her head and trudges over to my dad. He scoops her up. Then he looks at us, each of us, up and down.

"What happened to you three?" he asks.

I guess we do look a little scruffy. Dirt. Grass stains. Messed-up hair with dried leaves and twigs in it.

"Touch football," Murph says with a smile. "Lurena tackled Dmitri."

Lurena smiles, too.

"On that foot?" Dad says, pointing at my boot.

"He's joking," I say. "We all fell down."

"We were playing 'Ring Around the Rosy,'" Murph says.

"Funny," Dad says, turning to leave. "Get to class."

It isn't till we're inside that we discover Fido had gotten away from him again. All my classmates are pressed up to the windows, laughing as Dad chases her around the playground, hunched over, his hands out, trying to catch her. He stumbles a couple times. He runs into a swing and gets tangled up. He bonks his head on the slide.

I know I should go out there and help him, but what I really want to do is to run away and hide.

6. A person can't run away with a broken foot.

This has not been a normal school day for me. On a normal school day, kids don't surround me every chance they get, telling me how lucky I am, asking me questions, and pestering me for favors. Normally, they barely notice me.

Lurena, who has always pestered me, has been pestering me overtime. Yeah, she defends me, but that's probably the worst thing a girl can do to a guy my age. It brought out even more meanness and rudeness than usual from Dmitri. In fact, today he's earned extra-credit points in meanness and rudeness.

It has been a bad day. A very bad day. A very, very bad day. Our teacher, Ms. Charp, always says not to use *very* twice in a row like that, but I bet she's never had the kind of day I've had. I'm having a very, very, *very* bad day. Take that, Ms. Charp.

When finally the last bell rings, Murphy and I—with a mob of kids following us—walk out to Dad's car. Well, Murph and the mob walk. I hobble. I'm a hobbler. A mobbed hobbler.

Dad didn't bring Fido this time. Smart man.

"You want me to come over for a while and help you get around?" Murphy asks.

"No thanks," I say. "You've helped enough." I climb into the car, slam the door, and, to Dad, say, "Drive."

He hits the gas—or electricity, or whatever—and the hybrid moves away without a sound. I've never enjoyed silence more.

At home, I hobble from the car to the house, hobble up the porch steps, hobble up the inside steps, hobble to my room, then drop my crutches and collapse onto my bed. I stare up at the glow-in-the-dark solar system my mom stuck to my ceiling when I was little. It's afternoon, so it isn't glowing. It's just a bunch of cheap, milky-green plastic blobs.

Fido was waiting for me at the door when I came in, by the way. Was she glad to see me or sorry for causing such chaos at school? Probably a little of both. I hobbled past her, and she followed me up here. She's now lying beside me, licking my fingers over and over with her little pink tongue. I start to relax for the first time all day.

There's a knock on the door.

Fido barks.

"Who's there?" I ask.

"Your friend is here to see you, Rufus," my dad says from the hall.

Friend? Which friend? I didn't invite anyone.

"Lurena!" Lurena calls.

Of course.

"We're taking a nap," I say. "I'm really tired from my first day back at school."

"I brought Sharmet with me," Lurena says. "To see Fido."

Fido growls. She wants to see, or maybe eat, the animal on the other side of the door.

Sharmet is Lurena's hamster. She pronounces it like *ballet*: *shar-MAY.* She used to have two hamsters, but, according to her, the other one, Amherst, died of old age. Both hamsters' names, Sharmet and Amherst, are anagrams of the word *hamster*. Scrambling words is something Lurena and I have in common. That and rodent ownership.

"May we come in, please, Rufus?" Dad asks. There's impatience in his voice. He wants to ditch Lurena with me and get back to work.

I don't want Lurena to come in. I didn't invite her. She just showed up. As usual. I wonder if she also brought her chinchilla, China C. Hill, whose name is an anagram of *chinchilla*. Lurena has a theme going with her pet names.

"We'll wait for you in the kitchen," Dad grunts, then more patiently says, "Come on, Lurena. I'll get you and your gerbil a snack."

"Oh, it's not a gerbil, Art," Lurena says. "She's a hamster. I named her Sharmet, which is an anagram of . . ."

Their voices fade away. Fido turns her head

and looks at me. Eagerly. She wants to see (eat) Sharmet.

"All right," I say, and sit up.

Fido runs up to Sharmet in the kitchen and growls, her round ears flattened, her tiny teeth bared. Sharmet climbs up Lurena's long purple sleeve. Sharmet is a hider. According to Lurena, all Sharmet ever does is hide, which does not make her a good "buddy" for China—which, I guess, is why Lurena left China C. at home.

"I'm thinking I might get a ground squirrel," Lurena says as Sharmet inches farther up her sleeve. The thing's shivering like crazy. Sharmet, I mean, not Lurena. "They have one in at Exotique. It's so cute I could die."

Do people really die from seeing cute things? Would it be a bad thing if those people died?

Exotique is a store that sells all kinds of strange pets: ground squirrels, teacup pigs, skunks, cockroaches, chinchillas. Yes, Lurena bought China C. there.

"You want a pet *squirrel*?" I ask.

"Squirrels are way more active than most domestic rodents. Except Fido, of course. Fido's special."

My special domestic rodent is at the moment spinning in a circle, trying to catch her own tail, though she doesn't have one. Chasing her own rear end is how she deals with frustration. Me, I like to ride my bike.

"Okay, Lurena," I say. "You have to leave now. I'm going on a bike ride."

"A bike ride? With that?" She points at my boot.

"I actually ride better with it," I lie. I haven't biked since the accident. "You don't have your bike with you, do you?"

"No," she says. "But I could run home and get it."

I was afraid of this. "No, I want to ride alone."

Lurena nods. She isn't listening. She's looking at Fido. More like inspecting her.

"What?" I ask.

"She's getting fat."

"I'm sure she is. Except for today's little

adventure, she's been stuck in the house since I hurt my foot. Plus, I sneak her a lot of table food."

Lurena frowns.

"Running alongside my bike will burn some calories," I say, and stand up. "Good-bye, Lurena."

She nods again. "Okay. I get it. I'm leaving. But you really should stop feeding her human food, Rufus. If she gets too fat, she'll get rodent liver disease."

"Is that really a thing?"

She tilts her head. "How well do I know rodents, Rufus?"

"Right. So it's exercise time for Fido. Come on, girl. Bike ride!"

Fido hops up and down. She loves bike rides as much as I do.

"And you're sure it's okay to ride a bike with that boot on?" Lurena asks.

"Of course it is," I say.

But I'm not.

7. Fido isn't too fat to fall through sewer grates.

That's one thing I learned on our bike ride. I also learned she can swim. And that she can hold on to a stick tight enough for me to hoist her up. And that a quick dip in a sewer makes a guinea pig smell awful. Like a pig, I guess. I've never smelled a real live pig, but if they smell half as bad as Fido did after her swim in the sewer, they must stink to high heaven. I made her run behind the bike the rest of the way.

Another thing I learned: riding a BMX while wearing a medical boot is dangerous. The boot rubbed on the road. The bike wobbled. I nearly died.

"Roof!" Murphy says when he sees me

wobbling up. "Did you forget your foot is broken?"

"Shut up and get a hose!" I yell. "And dog shampoo! No questions! Do it now!"

He laughs, then runs to the spigot and twists it. I ride to the end of the hose, which is lying across the lawn like a long green snake. I drop my bike, grab the spray nozzle, and shoot a stream of water at Fido. It hits her in the face and sends her somersaulting backward.

"Don't drown her," Murphy says, running toward Fido with a bottle of shampoo.

Fido looks like a drowned rat. She looks up gloomily through her dripping fur.

"I think she's good and wet," Murphy says. "Ready for the wash cycle?" He squeezes a glob of shampoo into his palm, then rubs it into Fido's wet coat. She squirms under his hands a little, then relaxes.

He laughs. "Was it a skunk?"

"Sewer. She scared me to death. She ran over a grate and just disappeared."

Murphy keeps laughing. Everything's funny to this guy.

"How'd you get her out?" he asks.

"I found a stick and lowered it down through the grate; she bit down on it, and I lifted her out."

"Seriously?" He scratches Fido's head. "You are the coolest guinea dog ever."

"Do you think there are more?"

He shrugs. "Even if there aren't, Fido's the coolest."

This doesn't make sense, but I let it go, and ask, "Can you go for a ride?"

"I can't believe you're riding a bike with that boot on."

"It's easy," I lie. "Come on. I need a nice long bike ride. Lurena came over again."

More laughter. "Okay. I'll go get Buddy."

"And you finished your homework, right?"

"What do you think?" He flashes a mischievous smile.

If he doesn't bring his grades up, he'll have to repeat fifth grade. He doesn't want that any more than I do, but unless I keep after him, it will happen. He's used to charming his way out of problems. He's good at it. Everybody loves Murphy, and everybody lets him slide. Everyone except Ms. Charp, that is. And me.

"I think you didn't do it," I say.

He laughs. No surprise there.

"It's not funny. You want to flunk?"

He stops smiling and fake-furrows his brow. "Yes, I do. I want to flunk. My goal is to spend the rest of my life in the fifth grade. I want to be the world's first fifty-year-old fifth grader. I'll make them buy me a desk that rocks. A rocking desk."

"Go get your homework. I'll help you with it. And let Buddy out so she and Fido can play till we're finished."

"But I told you, I want—"

"Save it, Smurph," I say, using the name I've called him since kindergarten. "Get the dog and the math."

He snaps to attention, and salutes me crisply. "Yes, suh!" he says, then pivots and marches toward the house like a soldier. He opens the door and calls, "Attention, Buddy! Fido is here for a playdate! Come here on the double!"

Buddy bounds out the door, down the steps,

and across the lawn. Buddy is the world's most perfect dog: big, black, muscular, fast, fun, smart, obedient, and loyal. If I could have a dog, she'd be the one I'd want.

Murphy once offered to trade Buddy for Fido. I didn't take him seriously, though. He likes to fool around. He says things all the time that aren't exactly true.

I wonder if he meant it.

Even if he did, Dad wouldn't have allowed me to do it.

What kind of crazy nut turns down a dog like Buddy?

My dad.

Buddy runs at us and starts licking the lather off Fido. I set her down and spray her gently with the hose. Buddy gets a little wet in the process.

"Here—spray this!" Murphy calls from the porch, holding up his homework. "I'll tell Ms. Charp there was a flood!"

I set the nozzle to FINE and squeeze the trigger. A thin line of water streams into Murphy's face.

"Hey!" he splutters. "You missed!"

"No, I didn't."

He drops his homework, gives a Tarzan yell, then wrestles the nozzle away from me.

All four of us end up soaked to the skin.

Glorious.

8. Our fun was ruined by a girl and her hamster.

Lurena rode up on her sparkly purple bike, Sharmet peeking from the flowery basket attached to her handlebars.

"Why are you guys all wet?" she asks.

"We're giving Fido a bath," I say, and point the nozzle at her. "Want one?"

"Don't you dare! Don't you dare!" she screams, and ducks her head behind her basket.

I don't dare, but not because she doesn't deserve it. She does, for barging in where she wasn't wanted. Again. No, I don't blast her with cold water because I don't want her to be a part of our wet fun. And I do not want to see her soaked to the skin. Blech.

"What do you want, Lurena?" I ask. "Why did you come here?"

"To give Sharmet a bath?" she says.

"Sure!" Murphy says. "The more the merrier!"

That's sort of his catchphrase.

Lurena lifts her trembling hamster out of the basket, and I pull the trigger to the hose and douse it. I get Lurena a little, too.

"Hey!" she squeals. "You could warn a person!"

"You're right," I say, "I could. But I don't always remember to. If you don't want to get wet, I suggest you leave."

"Okay, I will," she says, taking off her frilly scarf and wrapping Sharmet in it. "I was just being friendly."

She looks hurt, which makes me feel bad. I don't hate her or anything. I didn't mind that she came over when I was laid up. It was boring being in bed all the time, even with a great pal like Fido around. Lurena and I played Scrabble, which was kind of fun, mostly because I usually won. But I can't have her dropping by whenever she feels like it. Or following me around. It's embarrassing. She's starting to act like a friend. I need to put a stop to it.

"Good," I say. "See you at school."

She frowns at me and puts her hamster back in her bike basket. "Thanks for giving Sharmet a bath. She hated it." Then she rides away.

"She likes you," Murphy says.

"I don't care," I say. Though I do. "Let's do your math so we can go for a ride."

"I'll do it when we get back."

I give him the Stony Stare.

"All right, *Art*," he says. "I'll do it now."

He gets some towels and we dry off, then we sit at the picnic table in his backyard. His dad has this huge silver gas grill that looks like what an astronaut would grill steaks on. He also has a workshop that he built himself and that's filled with tons of tools, including a band saw, a table saw, and a lathe. He made a playhouse for Murphy and his little sister, A.G., and a tree house, and a huge play structure with two swings, two slides, climbing ropes, and sliding poles. He even built the picnic table we're sitting on. His dad likes building things and fixing things. He even fixed my foot. He's a podiatrist.

Murphy not only has the best-ever dog, he has the best-ever dad.

My dad doesn't have a workshop or build and fix things. He has a toolbox and a workbench in the garage, but they're always covered with cobwebs. He calls someone if something is broken. He never barbecues. He's an editor for a golf e-zine, so mostly he sits at his computer in his gray suit and fuzzy slippers, moving his fingers and his lips, sighing and groaning.

"Mom says you have to stop fooling around and do your homework," A.G. says, busting out the back door. She's in her pajamas because she stayed home from school today. Again. She pretends she's sick a lot.

"You tell her that's exactly what I'm doing," Murphy says, holding up his math book.

"What disease do you have now?" I ask.

"Mom thinks it's just allergies, but I looked up my symptoms online, and I'm pretty sure it's tonsillitis. So I'll be checking into the hospital pretty soon, for a tonsillectomy."

"Gee, sis," Murphy says. "That's terrible. Will you still be able to talk?"

"Not for a while, I'm afraid." She shakes her head, tragically.

"Then I guess Mom will have to remind me herself to do what I'm already doing," Murphy says, with a toothy smile.

A.G. scowls and goes back inside. Murphy has the worst-ever little sister.

Right about then, Buddy races by. Fido follows a bit later, struggling to keep up. For a guinea pig, she's fast. But compared to Buddy . . .

"You know, sometimes I wish I had an ordinary dog," I say.

"But you have an *extra*ordinary dog," Murphy answers. "Everybody wants a dog like Fido."

"I know. That's part of the problem. Today was terrible. I've never gotten so much attention in my life."

"What's wrong with attention?"

I forget for a second that I'm talking to Murphy Molloy, the supreme master of attention getting. He loves it. He's not going to understand how it makes it hard for me to breathe. Or speak.

"It's not even me they're interested in. It's Fido. She's the attraction. I'm just her handler."

"So take this chance and let everybody get to know you," Murphy says. "You're a good guy. A *great* guy. Why do you want to hide it?"

"Of course you think that. We've been friends since we were little."

"I think it because it's true. Look at Lurena. She likes you, too."

"I don't care," I say again, but then I wonder, *Does she?* Isn't it just Fido—and maybe anagramming—that she finds interesting about me? Were we friends before Fido? No. Are we friends now?

I hope not.

Right?

I honestly don't know how I feel about it.

Buddy and Fido return, and Buddy sets her

head on Murphy's lap. Fido sets hers on my boot.

"A normal dog would definitely be better," I say, ending the discussion. "Now do your math."

"Aye, aye, Captain," Murphy says, as he leans down and scratches Fido's head. "Hey, is it me or is Fido getting kind of chubby?"

9. What I Would Do if I Were Presidog of the United States of America.

(Based on a very, very creative prompt assigned by Ms. Charp.)

- Give all kids with broken bones three months off school.
- Give all kids with broken bones a dog.
- Give all kids a dog.
- Own as many dogs as I want.
- Change the name of the White House to the Dog House.
- Change "President" to "Presidog."
- Make it illegal for fathers to refuse to give their sons dogs.
- Make it twice as illegal for mothers to

bring home strange rodents instead of dogs.

- Make asking questions about or begging for guinea dogs a federal offense punishable by ninety days of listening to Lurena tell you everything she knows about rodents.
- Lock up all people who go where they aren't invited.
- Lock up all people who try to catch other people's pets with a butterfly net (for example, Dmitri).
- Declare war on Dmitri.
- Make Lurena U.S. ambassador to Jupiter.
- Have the military custom-build an armor suit for me that prevents all broken bones, and, while they're at it, build me the best bike ever, then . . .
- Quit, because I hate being a celebrity.

My week has not gone well. It's gone very, very, very, very bad.

If Murphy's right and I'm a great guy, why don't I feel great? I feel the opposite of great. I feel bad. Very, very, very, very.

A lot of uninvited guests have come snooping around my house, knocking on the door, driving my dad crazy, driving me crazy, *acting* crazy. One kid climbed up the tree outside my bedroom window, hoping to take pictures of the guinea dog, but all he saw was me spelling out angry words with my Scrabble tile collection. He took pictures anyway, then asked me for money in exchange for not showing them to my mom. Another kid brought over his pet iguana and wanted to trade. I told him to get the angry word out of here. Another one wanted me to exchange his sugar packet collection for Fido. I was tempted. I like sugar a whole lot. But I said no thanks.

Dmitri really did try to catch Fido with a butterfly net. What a dope. Even if he'd caught her, she would have chewed her way out. And he didn't catch her.

Lurena still has not caught on that I don't want her dropping by all the time. I mean, she drops by *all* the time. You'd almost think she lived here. It's like a nightmare I can't wake up from. And I still think all she's interested in is Fido. Fido, Scrabble, and telling me interesting facts about rodents. Who knew chinchillas grow more than fifty hairs out of each follicle, while humans only grow one? And who *cares*? She really wants our rodents to become friends. Unfortunately, Fido really wants to eat Sharmet and China C.

Murphy keeps telling me I'm lucky to have Fido, and I still like her and all, but more and more I've been wishing things would return to normal. I want a normal dog. I want Fido to be a normal guinea pig. I want to go back to not being noticed.

And I have an idea that might make it all come true.

10. Maybe you can unteach a dog tricks.

I take Fido out to the backyard and, like usual, she finds a stick and carries it to me in her mouth. She wants to play Fetch. I don't usually say no to her, but I'm thinking I should start. Maybe if I stop encouraging her to act like a dog, she'll stop acting like one.

When I don't take the stick, she starts whining.

"No Fetch," I say.

She drops the stick, sits down in the grass, and whines louder.

"Quiet!" I say.

She obeys. Such a good . . . rodent.

I should probably stop using commands with her, too.

She runs away and returns with a piece of twine in her mouth.

"No Tug-of-War, either," I say.

She starts to whine. I give her the Stony Stare. She stops. Maybe I can use the stare to replace "Quiet!" Like Dad does.

She drops the twine in the grass, turns, and walks sadly away. She peeks back over her shoulder a couple of times to show me her sad eyes. You have to be firm and consistent when saying no. I heard Dad say that once when Mom suggested they get me "just a little dog, like a Chihuahua."

Fido returns, dragging her rubber flying ring through the grass.

"And no Catch."

She drops it and looks up at me like I'd said I hated her and wanted her to go away forever.

"Get used to it. You're not a dog, and the sooner you stop acting like one, the sooner my life can get back to normal."

Normal, meaning dogless.

I can't win.

I decide it's okay to scratch her head—people probably scratch their guinea pig's heads—and she wags her butt and rolls over so I can rub her belly, when suddenly we are attacked by a big black puffball of death.

It races around the corner, huffing and puffing, with its bluish tongue hanging out of its black mouth. Its name is Mars, it's a chow, and it belongs to my worst friend, Dmitri Sull.

If I ever get an actual dog, I wouldn't want it to be like Mars. He's puffy, for one thing. I mean, if you want puffy, get a cat. Mars is also highly prone to unpredictably aggressive behavior. That's what Ms. Charp said anyway when Dmitri brought Mars to school on Pet Day. She sent Mars home. That was a good day.

The puffball runs right to Fido, barking and snarling. Fido jumps to her feet and stares him down. He whimpers and starts sniffing her instead.

When they first met, I worried Mars might eat her, but (obviously) he didn't. Like Murph, Fido's good at making friends. For her, the more dogs the merrier. Even when the dogs are big black puffballs of death.

This time, though, she's not in the mood for company. I know how she feels. She looks away from Mars and jumps into my lap.

"Rufus, old pal!" Dmitri says.

I'm not his old pal, and we both know it.

Fido growls at him. She has good instincts—with people, anyway. I don't get why she likes Mars.

"What's with her?" Dmitri asks.

"Maybe she doesn't like uninvited guests," I answer. "I know I don't." This sounds mean coming out of my mouth, but I really am fed up with party crashers.

Dmitri pretends he doesn't hear me and pulls his fancy phone out of his pants pocket.

"I'm going to shoot some videos of Fido doing tricks and upload them to the Internet."

"Oh, you *are*, are you? You'll need my permission for that, won't you?"

"I doubt it," he says, narrowing his eyes into a threat.

"Well, I won't give you permission. I don't

want strangers gawking at Fido. She's not a freak or something."

"She isn't?"

I'd like to wipe that smirk off his face. I'd like to smack it off. I know what this is about. Dmitri is used to getting what he wants. Fancy, expensive phones, for example. Since he can't have Fido, he figures he'll be the guy who makes her famous. He'll attach his name to the videos and take credit for introducing the world to the one and only guinea pig that acts like a dog—the guinea dog!

Not on my watch.

"No, she isn't. And I won't let you treat her like a freak. So put away the phone and get lost. And take your puffball with you."

We are both surprised. I don't usually stand up for myself. This isn't about me, though. It's about Fido. Which makes it easier for some reason.

I can see by the way he's glaring at me that he's trying to think of a mean comeback. All he comes up with, though, is "Fine!" Then he stomps off. The puffball trots after him.

Fido climbs up to my chin and licks it. She's glad Dmitri's gone, too. I'd sure like to have some fun with her right now, maybe work off some of her fat, but I know the only way to stop kids from acting like Dmitri just did is to stop treating her like a dog, and to start treating her like a guinea pig.

I walk over to her doghouse. It's so small, I can carry it with one hand. I pick it up.

"This is for your own good," I tell her, though I'm not entirely sure it is. Anyway, I dump her house in the garage and shut the door.

11. "You'd whine, too, if you were in jail."

This is what I say when my dad asks why Fido is whining during dinner.

"She's getting fat from eating table food," I go on. "So she has to stay in her cage during meals until she slims down."

I don't like telling fibs, but I'd like to keep my parents out of this.

Dad looks up at the ceiling—Fido's up in my room—and frowns. "I don't know if I can properly digest my food with that sound."

"She'll stop," I say. "You can't give in to a pet's whining or she'll think that's all she has to do to get what she wants. You must be firm and consistent."

"That's very wise," Mom says with a proud

smile. "You'll make a good parent someday."

"Will *not*!" Like I'll ever have kids! Don't you have to have a wife for that? Not on your life.

"Well, if we are going to let this noise persist, I'm going to fetch some earplugs," Dad says, rising from his chair.

"That's not very polite," Mom replies.

"Neither would be indigestion. Excuse me."

He heads for his study, where he keeps his supply of earplugs. He bought a box of them after Mom bought Fido.

"How was your first week back at school?" Mom asks.

"Fine."

If I tell her how awful it really was, she'll get all gooey and comforty, and that will only make things worse. I might even cry. That's what mom-love does to me: makes me a baby again.

"Your dad said Dmitri came by to see you."

"Yeah," I say, and leave it at that.

"And Lurena? Did she visit again?"

She makes a twinkly face, the one she always makes when Lurena is mentioned. It makes me very uncomfortable.

"Amazingly, no. She must have been in a horrible accident."

"Rufus!"

"Sorry. I was joking. It's just that she comes over all the time, even though I never invite her."

"Lurena is a good friend," Mom says. Twinkle, twinkle.

Dad returns, orange foam earplugs poking out of his ears. He points to them to make sure we understand he can't hear anything we say.

"You should invite her to your birthday party," Mom says.

I wish Dad had brought me some earplugs.

"Your foot should be pretty much healed by then," Mom says. "I think we'll have a backyard party, with games, maybe a piñata?"

What am I, six?

"I don't know . . . ," I say.

"You can invite all your friends. Murphy, Lurena, Dmitri . . ."

"Dmitri?"

"I know you haven't gotten along with him

very well in the past, but I think he's really making an effort. He visited you when you were laid up and a few times since."

He was just being nice because he wants Fido. And for Dmitri, nice is still pretty mean. I don't say this to Mom, though. I don't want her trying to help. Her idea of help is inviting Lurena to join our family picnic. Or inviting her and Dmitri to my birthday party. Or having a piñata at my birthday party. Or bringing home a guinea pig instead of a dog.

"Anyway," she says, "I mailed out the invitations today. Lurena helped me with the list."

"What?" I ask so loudly even Dad jumps. So she was suggesting I invite Lurena and Dmitri even though she had already mailed them invitations? How treacherous can you get!

"I called her from work," Mom says.

"You know her *phone number*?"

"She said you've become quite popular at school, and she gave me a list of kids I could potentially invite."

"I don't want a big party, Mom," I say,

knowing that what I want doesn't always get through to her. Like when I wanted a dog . . .

"Oh, it won't be big. I just invited Lurena, Murphy, and Dmitri. I'm thinking we'll have it the Saturday before your birthday. I'll take care of everything. Don't you worry."

Don't me worry? Lurena and Dmitri are coming. I'll have only a week to de-doggify Fido.

Fido whined all through dinner. Afterward, I try to make it up to her by letting her out of her cage and playing with her for a while. I don't play with her like she's a dog. I can't play with her like she's a guinea pig, because I don't know how.

She bites down on my pant leg and tries to tug me toward the front door.

"Guinea pigs don't go on walks," I say, but it doesn't stop her.

I put her back in her cage.

She whines, and I gave her the Stony Stare. She keeps whining. She whines and whines and whines. So I go downstairs and sneak into my dad's study.

12. Yes, I wore earplugs to bed that night.

They kept me awake as much as Fido did. Earplugs make my head feel like it's suffocating. True, I don't breathe through my ears, but air does pass through them. At some point during the night I took them out.

Fido's whining got louder. I hoped Dad wore earplugs to bed.

I woke up exhausted.

"She didn't stop whining, Rufus," Dad says when I walk into the kitchen in the morning. "Did you keep her in her cage all night?"

"I didn't mean to," I lie. "I . . ."

I had to come up with another fib, which is the problem with telling them. They multiply. Like rabbits. Or guinea pigs.

"I fell asleep," I say, which, of course, I didn't. I couldn't. "I was really tired. I mean, this week has been really strenuous."

Strenuous was a word Mom used about my first day back: "Oh, honey, such a strenuous day for you!"

Dad buys it. My parents can be so easy to fool. I guess that's because they trust me.

Ooh, that doesn't feel good.

"Sorry she kept you awake," I say.

After I eat my eggs and sausages, I go back to my room to feed Fido. She gets guinea pig pellets, whether she likes them or not. She tries to make a break for it when I open the cage door.

"Oh no, you don't," I say, shoving her back in. "You're a guinea pig, and guinea pigs live in cages."

She whimpers and gives me big, sad, puppy eyes.

"Stop that. You think I like this? You have to quit acting like something you're not. You're not a dog, okay? You're a guinea pig. So act like one. Stop whining. Guinea pigs don't whine."

Or do they?

She sinks to the floor of her cage, sets her chin on her front paws, and gazes up at me like I'm the meanest pet owner in the universe. I feel like I am.

"Be good and when I get home I'll take you out of your cage for a while. Okay?"

She takes a deep breath, which makes her puff up even fatter than usual, and lets it out. Then she starts whining again.

I know she won't be quiet if I leave her in the cage all day, that she'll drive Dad crazy and he'll come up and let her out. So I look her in the eyes, and say, "I'll let you out, but you have to stay in my room. You can't run around the house. And you have to be quiet. Understand?"

I swear she nods.

I open the cage door, and she shoots out like a bullet—a chubby, furry bullet. She tears around the room, leaping and barking. I don't know if I've ever seen her so happy, not even with Buddy.

After a few laps around the room, she charges me. I'm squatting, so she nearly knocks me over. She *is* getting heavy. She licks my hands and my arms. She climbs up on my knees and licks my face.

"Stop it!" I say. "Down!"

She obeys instantly.

Oops. That was a command. This is hard.

"Be a good girl, okay? I'll see you after school."

Her tongue flops out, and her head starts bobbing.

I stand up and leave the room, shutting the door tightly behind me. I hear no whining, so I hobble downstairs.

Dad meets me at the front door.

"She stopped," he says. "Good."

"I let her out of her cage," I say. "But I want her to stay in my room today."

"Why?" Dad asks, suddenly suspicious.

It's fibbing time again. Oh, dear.

"I want her to get some rest. She didn't sleep all night."

I'm getting better at lying.

Which worries me.

13. "Dude, I need you to train my guinea pig."

This is what Dmitri says to me when I take a seat on Monday morning. We sit next to each other in class. Just my luck. "I bought a guinea pig, and I want you to train it to act like a dog."

"I don't know how to do that," I say. I wasn't the one who trained Fido to act the way she does. In fact, I had spent the entire weekend trying to train her to act like a guinea pig and had gotten nowhere. I'm no animal trainer. "I told you, Fido was the way she was when we got her."

"I know what you told me," Dmitri snarls. "But I looked up Petopia online, and guess what? It doesn't exist. You made it up because you don't want anyone to have a guinea dog except you."

I look at him, with his sharp nose and his sharp chin and his sharp tongue and his eyes shooting daggers at me. The kid's face could cut you.

"No, I didn't," I say, and look away.

"Yes, you *did*," he says loudly. "And you're going to train my guinea pig to act like a dog . . . or else!"

The rest of the kids turn and look at us. Some whisper to one another.

Linus Axelbrig says, "Can you train my guinea pig, too, Rufus?"

Then Shireen Hourani says, "Mine, too!"

I hadn't realized how popular guinea pigs were.

Everybody is firing me questions, asking for favors, giving me advice, making me offers. It all blends into the sound of a herd of squirrels chattering. Okay, not a herd, but what do you call a bunch of squirrels? A pack? A squad? A squadron? A squirrel squadron?

The squadron moves in closer. I don't like it.

I need Murphy, but, of course, he's late. I ask myself what he would do in this situation.

Probably stand up on a chair and quiet everyone down with a big smile, then invent some wild story that would shut them up by making them laugh. And he'd have fun doing it, too.

Why is it so easy for Murphy to be relaxed and funny? Why doesn't he freeze up when he's talking to a group of people? How does he always know what to say?

Why can't I be like him?

If I could be like him, maybe Fido being a guinea dog wouldn't be a problem. Maybe it would be a good thing.

I mean, it *is* a good thing. I *like* that she acts like a dog. So does Murphy. So why does it have to change?

Because I can't change. I can't be like Murphy. I can't love the attention. I can't stand it.

Since I can't be like him and charm chattering crowds, I stare at my feet and wait for him to show up. Or, if not him, Ms. Charp. She's out of the room making copies.

The squirrels tighten around me. I can't breathe. I might scream.

Instead, Lurena does. "There is *too* a Petopia!"

Everyone shuts up.

"His mom told me so," Lurena says.

I'm not happy that she feels the need to tell everyone she knows my mom. It makes it seem as if she's a close friend, not only of mine, but of my whole family. My mom may adore her and invite her over no matter what I say about it, but that does not make her my friend, or my sister.

Sister! What a dreadful, dreadful thought!

"She said she bought Fido there, then it disappeared." She pauses to look around the room, before adding, "Into thin air."

No one makes a sound.

"And she doesn't lie," Lurena goes on.

Unlike me.

"Rufus told me he didn't train Fido, and I believe him. Besides, he wouldn't have had time to. Fido was a guinea dog when Raquel bought her."

I cringe. Did she really just call my mom by her first name? I know Murph calls my dad

Art, but that's because he's my best friend. And a guy. What will people think Lurena is to me?

"There's only one guinea dog in Rustbury, so don't bother looking for another one," she says. "And Roof can't train your guinea pigs to act like dogs." (Yeah, she called me Roof, like Murph does.) "So stop bothering him. Leave him alone."

She glares into each squirrel's eyes. She glares the longest into Dmitri's. Her eyes look wild, like she's a witch or a vampire or insane.

Some kids snicker. Dmitri laughs out loud.

"Dude, why does this freaky girl always fight your fights for you?"

A couple of boys snort. Which makes me angry. Which is weird.

"Freaky? That's the pot calling the kettle black," Lurena says.

This gets puzzled expressions from everyone, including me.

"What?" Dmitri asks, and laughs harder. It reminds me of the way villains laugh in movies when they have the superhero tied up and they're explaining their evil plans to take over the world. Dmitri would play a good movie villain. Or even a real one.

Where the heck is Ms. Charp anyway? Is it really okay for a teacher to leave her classroom unattended while a riot is going on?

Suddenly, without meaning to, I stand up. Too fast. I knock my desk over and it hits the floor. It seems, even to me, that I'm standing up to Dmitri, for Lurena. Which I'm not. I'm just clumsy.

Everyone is staring at me, waiting to see what I'll do next. Slap Dmitri's face with a glove, maybe. I don't have a glove, or a clue what to do next.

"Sorry," Ms. Charp says as she *finally* hustles into the room and drops a tall stack of papers on her desk. "Long line in the copy room."

Everyone sits down. Everyone except Lurena and me. She helps me lift my desk. Then we sit down.

The bell rings. Murphy breezes in—just in time to be officially late—and blurts out, "So did everyone hear about the hairy frogs with claws!"

14. Ten reasons a rodent can't replace a dog.

1. People with pet rodents will think you have something in common.
2. People with pet rodents will want you to train them. (Their rodents, I mean.)
3. Some of these rodent lovers will be girls.
4. Some of these rodent lovers will be bullies.
5. They will all pay way too much attention to you.
6. They may come to your house uninvited.
7. Rodents look like rodents, even if they fetch.
8. Rodents smell like rodents.
9. Rodents are rodents.
10. Rodents aren't dogs.

This is what I'm thinking as I make my way down the hall after the final bell. I look at the floor, not wanting to make eye contact with anyone. I also have orange earplugs that I swiped from my dad's stash stuffed into my ears. I point to them if someone comes up to me, and mouth, *Can't hear you.*

One of these people is Lurena, who wants to get Fido and Sharmet together after school. Like for a playdate. A playdate for rodents.

Can't hear you, I mouth.

At the car, Dad asks me a question, but I can't hear it.

"What?" I yell.

He taps his ear.

"Oh!" I yell, and take out the earplugs.

"Is she with you?" he asks immediately. Kind of urgently. He seems worried. Which scares me. And confuses me.

"Lurena?" I ask. She's the only "she" who comes to mind, probably because I just saw her.

"I didn't hear her anymore," Dad says, "so

I went up to your room to see if she was okay. And she wasn't there."

And I get who the "she" is. I feel prickles on the back of my neck.

"She's probably just hiding."

"No," he says, and puts the car in gear. It rolls silently forward. "I searched your room. You really should clean it someday. Some of the things I found still haunt me."

I knew that was coming. He doesn't call my room the Dump for nothing.

"I'll look for her when I get home."

"Be my guest, but I'm telling you, she isn't in your room."

"Then you must have let her out."

"No," he says, "I did not."

He seems more annoyed now than worried, and I'm annoyed *and* worried, and I sure wish he'd drive faster than the speed limit for once.

He doesn't. He comes to a full and complete stop at every stop sign and looks in all directions before proceeding into the intersection. This is what he has told me all drivers should do, and most do not.

It takes a full and complete eon to get home.

If it weren't for the medical boot, I would bolt from the car to the house and zoom up the steps to my room. Instead, I struggle to get out of the car and speed-hobble to the house. This takes another eon.

When at last I'm in my room, I call, "Here, Fido! Here, girl! Come, Fido! Come!"

I know I'm using commands, but this is an emergency.

She doesn't come.

"Speak!" I say. It's worth a try. "Speak, Fido!"

She doesn't.

I search my bed first, then I start piling stuff from the floor onto it: dirty clothes, comic books, shoes, empty chip bags, dried gum, pebbles, a pinecone, a Frisbee, a pink rubber ball with guinea-pig-tooth marks in it, wadded-up notebook paper, a foam football with guinea-pig-tooth marks in it, Scrabble tiles, a corn cob, a sticky sucker stick with guinea-pig-tooth marks in it, and a moldy, stiff PBJ with guinea-pig-tooth marks in it. I don't see how any of this could haunt someone. My dad can be like Murphy: an exaggerator.

After everything is off the floor, I dig out all the stuff from under the bed, then all the stuff from under my dresser. I pile it all onto the heap, which is now up to my chin.

My dad appears in the doorway behind me. "Any luck?"

I shake my head. "She *must* have sneaked out when you opened the door."

He looks offended. "I was exceedingly careful not to let that happen. Ex*ceed*ingly."

"Did anyone else come in here? Mom, maybe?"

"She's been at work all day."

"Then how did Fido get out?" I yell. Much too loud.

He taps his foot and Stony-Stares me.

"Sorry," I say, and take a breath. "Did you search the whole house?"

"Yes."

"So what are you saying? That she got out of the *house*?"

"That's what I'm saying."

He's acting calm. Acting. I can tell he's worried about this. He has been since I got into the car. He doesn't want me to know he's worried, so he's pretending to be annoyed, haunted, and insulted. This is classic Dad. He knows if I know he's worried, I will freak out, which I'm kind of doing anyway. That's because I know he's worried.

This is getting me nowhere.

"I'll search the house again, if that's okay," I say. I get the feeling he wasn't very thorough, but I don't want to say so. He already got upset when I suggested he hadn't searched my room thoroughly.

"Suit yourself," he says.

"Did you check the garage?" It's connected to the house, with a door into the kitchen. Maybe it got left open.

"Yes. She isn't in there. By the way, why is her doghouse in there?"

"Why does it matter?" I scream.

I'm in no mood to concoct a fib. I know Fido was upset with me for putting her doghouse away, for not playing with her, for keeping her in the cage, for treating her like a rodent (which she is), but it suddenly occurs to me that maybe she was upset enough to . . .

"I'm sorry I'm screaming!" I scream. "But will you just help me find her?!"

15. I turn the house upside down.

No Fido.

Dad flashes me an I-told-you-so look.

We search the yard, the bushes, under the porch. No Fido.

I walk out to the curb in front of our house and lean on my crutches, scanning the cul-de-sac. She could be anywhere. Hiding in a neighbor's hedge. Or in a garden. Or under someone else's porch. Or anywhere in the whole wide world.

Could she really have run away? Was she that upset? Did she feel I no longer wanted her? No longer liked her? No longer loved her?

Is it possible to love a rodent?

Do I?

Mom's hybrid turns the corner and pulls into the driveway. I hobble over to it.

"Your dad called," she says, as she climbs out of her car. "I take it by your long face you haven't found her."

"They let you leave work just because our pet guinea pig is missing?"

"No, honey," she says, placing her hand on my shoulder. "I waited till my shift was over at five."

"Is it already *five*?" I shriek.

"I'm sure we'll find her," she says, and gives me a hug.

I like it, but I'd rather she didn't do it out here in the open.

I wriggle free. "Do you think she ran away from home?"

She smiles. "Of course not. Why would she? She's happy here. She loves you. You take good care of her."

My heart sinks. "I don't know. Maybe I don't."

She tries to hug me again, but I twist

away and get snarled in my crutches. Mom props me back up.

"Don't worry," she says. "She'll turn up. You'll see."

I want to tell her that I had been trying to untrain Fido, to treat her like a guinea pig (which she is), but I decide to keep my mouth shut and see if she's right about Fido's showing up. My gut tells me she isn't, that Fido won't be back.

Because of my gut, I can't eat my dinner. Which is unusual. I usually eat seconds, sometimes thirds. After the dishes are done, I go out to the backyard and call Fido till Dad says I have to come in. Then I call her from my bedroom window till Dad says I have to be quiet.

I hear my mom on the phone, calling the neighbors, asking them to be on the lookout for an orange guinea pig with a white mohawk. That's when I get the idea to hang some posters around the neighborhood. My dad helps me design one on his computer—he's good at making signs—then prints out a stack of them.

It says LOST GUINEA PIG, and it has a picture of Fido and our contact information.

"I'll hang them tomorrow," Dad says. "Better get to bed. It's late. School tomorrow."

"I'm not sure I feel very good," I say, with my hand on my stomach, like it doesn't feel very good. Actually, it *doesn't* feel very good.

"I think that's hunger. And worry."

"Maybe." I look up at him. I want to tell him about how I treated Fido, too, but just say, "Good night."

Mom comes up to tuck me in. I've been telling her I don't need her to do that anymore, that I'm too old for it, but tonight I don't mind. She has a chicken leg wrapped in a cloth napkin.

"I don't know if it's the chicken's left or right leg," she says.

It's a family joke, something I asked when I was little: "Is this the chicken's left leg or its right?" Mentioning it usually makes me smile. Not tonight.

"You really should eat. I'm sure Fido would want you to."

I'm not sure she would, but I take the drumstick and bite into the tender, juicy meat. Which gives me a scary thought.

"You don't think Fido went outside and a cat got her, do you? Or a dog?" That would be ironic. Ironic and horrific.

"She can take care of herself," Mom says.

That's true. Fido stands up to big dogs like Buddy and Mars. But I'm not sure about cats.

I don't finish the chicken. Mom wraps it up again in the napkin.

"Get some sleep now," she says, and shuts out the light.

"But where will Fido sleep tonight? Outside?"

I think about creatures that come out at night. Owls. Bears. Werewolves. Cats.

"She'll be fine," Mom says. "She's probably found some nice hiding place. And she's got her fur to keep her warm."

"If she hasn't already been flattened by a truck," I say, coming up with yet another horrible fate for my little friend. Why am I being so imaginative all of a sudden? That's Murph's territory, not mine.

"She hasn't been flattened. Now good night, sweetie." She goes out, pulling the door shut behind her, but not closing it all the way. For Fido, I suppose, when she returns. If she returns.

"We left the doggie door open, too," Mom whispers.

She brought one home from work last week and installed it herself. She does most of the handiwork around here.

I hear her bare feet walk along the carpeted hall and down the stairs. Then it's dark and quiet. Soon my eyes adjust, and I see a beam of glowing light coming in my window and landing on Fido's cage. Her empty cage.

I climb out of bed, pull open the window, kneel on the carpet, and press my nose against the cold screen.

"Come on, Fido!" I whisper-call. "Fido, come home!"

16. I'm not in the mood to hear about hairy, clawed frogs.

But Murphy keeps telling me about them anyway.

"When they feel threatened, they break their own toes, which poke through their skin, and become—you'll never believe it—*claws*!"

Come on, Murphy. A frog with hair isn't bizarre enough without having to add claws made of broken toes? What's with the hard sell?

Which leads me to wonder if it's really true. Nothing is weirder than nature. Look at the platypus. Or Fido. But Murphy enjoys playing around with the truth. He loves convincing me that a made-up thing is real (once he got me to believe that poisonous ducks had descended on Rustbury) and convincing me that a real thing is made up (for example, polar bears have black skin).

I wonder what I would have said if he had told me about a guinea pig that obeys commands, plays Fetch, and runs alongside your bike—a "guinea dog." I'm pretty sure I wouldn't have believed him. Then again, Murphy is a champion persuader.

So I listen to him talk about the hairy frog as we walk to school, even though I'm not in the mood. I told Dad I didn't want a ride today, that I could make it on foot. I don't have my crutches, even. Walking with the medical boot has gotten easier. I use the weight of it to propel me forward, then set it down lightly, and push off hard with the other foot. I probably look like Captain Hook, but at least it works. And Murphy's with me, in case I fall on my face, or butt.

"The problem is, they're not only acting in self-defense anymore," he says. "They're going on the offensive. Slashing up fish in the lake. Slashing ducks."

"Poisonous ducks?" I ask.

"No, regular ducks." My sarcasm doesn't slow him down. "You know the guy who works at the roller rink? The guy with the cobra tattoo on his neck? They got his Chihuahua. Cut him up pretty bad. We should go to the lake and see if we can find one. I've seen pictures of them online, and they're freaky. They have hair growing around their waists, like they're wearing hula skirts."

"Murph?" I interrupt, and point to my boot.

"Oh, right. We'd never get there and back in time for school. We'll go after."

"I'm going to look for Fido after school."

Murphy slaps his forehead. "Ack! Of course you are! I mean, *we* are. I'll help you."

"My dad made this great poster. He's out hanging them all over the neighborhood."

I pull one of them out of my bag. Dad asked me to pass some out at school, but I'm not going to. I know kids will make a big fuss, and I don't need more fuss than I'm already getting. Plus, I don't want kids who want a guinea dog to go looking for Fido, and maybe find her, and keep her. Finders keepers, and all that.

"Cool!" Murphy says.

"Yeah, my dad makes cool posters," I say, then try to think of other cool things he makes. It's not easy. He doesn't make a lot of things. He makes good pie, but I'm not sure that qualifies as cool.

"I'm sure someone will see Fido and call," Murph says.

"I don't want anyone at school to know she's missing, okay, Murph?"

"Really? Why not? They can help look for her. The more eyes the merrier, you know?"

"Believe me, if they see her, I'll hear about it. But mostly it'll just mean—"

"More attention. I get it."

"Yeah, I'm getting enough."

"You can't get enough attention."

"*You* can't, you mean. I can. I'm sick to death of it."

Murphy shakes his head. "You're crazy, but all right. My lips are sealed."

Yeah, right. Like they ever stay that way.

17. DMITRI = DIMWIT.

Almost.

The guy doesn't know right from wrong. Or he does and doesn't care. He does wrong all the time, like he has special permission to, like he's better than everyone else. Which he isn't. He's worse.

He's been telling everyone he shot secret videos of Fido doing tricks with his fancy, expensive phone. I think he's lying. I never saw him shoot Fido doing anything dog-like, but maybe he hid in the bushes when I was trying to train the dog out of her. She acted like a dog anyway. Maybe he got that on video.

Whether he did or not, I get extra mobbed at school. It's as if I'm a drop of blood and my classmates are sharks. Ravenous sharks. I'm actually a drop of blood with a broken foot. So I can't get away.

"I can't wait to see the video!"

"Did you give Dmitri permission?"

"Did you bring Fido to school?"

"You should *breed* it!"

"Is Dmitri going to post it online?"

Oh, man, I hope not. I don't want the whole world to know about Fido.

"All right, break it up! Break it up!" Murphy says, locking my arm and pulling me through the crowd. I keep up the best I can with my ball-and-chain boot. "Go about your business! This is an unlawful assembly! Move away from the celebrity! Give him room! Let us through! Beep, beep!"

The crowd stays with us all the way to the doors of the school. How do superstars stand this?

Luckily, the bell rings. Like magic, everyone scatters and goes on their way.

"Thanks," I say to Murphy, "but you do realize this means you're going to be on time to class?"

"The price I pay for keeping the peace."

"I'm afraid I'm going to have to murder Dmitri and his phone."

"As a peace officer, I have to warn you that, if you do, it is my sworn duty to prosecute you to the fullest extent of the law. But—off the record—I won't blame you."

"I'll keep that in mind."

Dimwit is waiting for me at my locker.

"You guys want to see the videos?" he asks, holding out his sleek, black phone, which is protected by a thick rubber case with a camo design. It's pretty cool, I must admit.

I'm sure everyone has been begging to see the videos, but does he really believe *I* would be interested in watching them?

Dimwit.

"Delete them," I say. "You don't have my permission."

"Who says I need it? I can shoot anything I want. And no way am I going to delete them. I'm going to post them."

He smirks at me, like he's totally won, but I'm just relieved he hasn't posted them yet.

"Have you uploaded them to your computer?"

"Not yet. Why?"

I glance at Murphy, and he gives me a wink.

"Got to get to class, boys," he says, snapping a salute. He walks away, but not toward the classroom. Toward the office.

Dmitri scoots after him, of course, calling, "Wait up, Murph!"

This should work out perfectly. He'll follow Murphy to the office; Murphy will pretend he wants to see the videos; Dimwit will take out his phone; and Tamra, the school secretary, who happens to adore Murphy (who doesn't?), will confiscate the phone. Phones aren't allowed at school.

I'd love to watch all this happen, but with the foot I won't have time. Murphy understands this. Plus, he doesn't mind if he's late. Or if Dmitri is.

Good old Murphy.

He'll find a way to get Dmitri to delete the videos, too, I bet. He could probably get Dmitri to flush his fancy phone down the toilet.

That's how charming Murph can be, and how desperate for Murph's attention Dmitri is.

When I sit down at my desk, Lurena says, "I heard about the videos. That Dmitri's got a lot of nerve. He can't get a guinea dog of his own, so he shows off with yours."

She should talk. She wants one, too. Everyone does.

Including me.

But I like that she thinks what Dmitri did stinks.

I'm tempted to tell her Fido is missing. Maybe she's had guinea pigs disappear on her before and would know where to look. Can I trust her not to tell everyone?

I doubt it.

The bell rings again, and everyone settles into their desks. Everyone but Murphy and Dmitri.

I lean over and, against my better judgment, whisper to Lurena, "Fido's missing."

18. I am never in the mood to hear about guinea pig bloat.

"Animals hide when they get sick," Lurena says. "And she was getting fat. My theory is she has guinea pig bloat."

"I told you she was stuck in my room the whole time I was laid up, and that she ate a lot of people food, like sausages, and pizza, and tuna-fish sandwiches."

"Where would a bloated, or just plain fat, guinea pig hide, Lurena?" Murphy asks.

Murphy and I walked home together. Lurena met us here after she stopped at her house to pick up her pet rodents. We're sitting in the backyard, where no one can see us. Lurena is holding a rodent in each hand, and nuzzling them.

Lurena shrugs. "Did you search the house?"

"Oh, gee, should I have?" I ask sarcastically. I'm amazed she'd ask such a stupid question.

"I mean, did you look *every*where? Your room is always a pigsty. I don't know how you ever find *any*thing, not to mention a poor, bloated guinea pig."

"She. Is. Not. Bloated. She ate too much. People do that every year on Thanksgiving, and no one dies. And I cleaned my room as I was searching. I looked under *every*thing. I looked *every*where."

"Okay, okay. So how do you think she escaped?"

"My dad must've let her out. He said he went in once to check on her because she was so quiet. Maybe she slipped out without his noticing."

"Why was the door shut?" Murphy asks. "You usually let Fido go wherever she wants."

I was worried this might come up. Murphy and Lurena both love Fido. How can I tell them that I've been trying to train her to be a plain old normal guinea pig? They'll think it was mean of me to keep her locked up, to try to change her.

"Especially since she's gotten fat," Murphy goes on. "Didn't you want her to exercise? You know, run up and down the stairs? Play Fetch with your dad?"

"Hey," Lurena says, twisting her head side to side, "where's Fido's doghouse?"

I might as well come clean. They're both too smart.

I tell them the truth.

"Why would you want her to act like a regular guinea pig?" Lurena asks.

Murphy nods. He's figured it out. But he doesn't tell Lurena. He'll wait and let me say it. Or not say it. He knows it's my choice. He's a good friend.

"Can we just find her?" I ask, and march away to one of my dad's flower beds. (Yeah, he not only cooks and cleans, he gardens, too.)

I pretend to look for Fido among the flowers, when really I'm just dodging Lurena's question.

I feel bad for . . .

1. Trying to de-doggify Fido. She can't help being what she is.
2. Denying her food.
3. Locking her in her cage, and in my room.
4. Ignoring her whines.
5. Dragging her doghouse into the garage.
6. Not letting her sleep with me.
7. Lying to my dad, my mom, my best friend, and even Lurena.
8. Driving away the pet I love.

"She's not out here," Lurena says. "Let's check the house."

"I told you. She's not in there. My dad and I both looked."

"Well, I haven't."

19. Lurena turns the house upside down.

It's like she owns the place. She opens doors, drawers, cabinets. She dives into closets, under sinks, under beds. Her long, frilly, old-fashioned dress gets pretty dusty.

Murphy and I keep an eye on her rodents. We sit with them on the living room floor. Sharmet, the hider, tries to climb inside my boot. She tries to shimmy up my pant leg. She tries to slip under my T-shirt. I block each invasion. I don't want a hamster in my clothes. She finally gives up and grooms herself on my knee.

I'm really glad Fido doesn't act like a rodent. If I find her, I'll stop trying to train the dog out of her.

If I find her.

"I love this chinchilla!" Murphy says. China C. is perched on his head, kneading his curly hair.

Lurena passes by and walks up to the door of Dad's study. She's about to knock.

"I wouldn't do that," I say.

She does.

"Who is it?" Dad answers sharply.

"It's me, Art. Lurena Shraits. I'm looking for Fido."

"She's not in here. I have work to do."

"It won't take a second," Lurena says, in a singsong voice.

"Oh, all right," he grunts. I hear him stand up, stomp to the door, and turn the knob. The door swings open. His face is clenched like a fist. "You have two minutes." He checks his watch.

"Thank you," Lurena sings as she steps by him. "That will be more than enough time."

Murphy and I stay in the hall, out of harm's way.

"She doesn't seem to be afraid of anything," Murphy says.

"Nope."

"I bet she'd be afraid of a hairy, clawed frog."

"Got one?"

He shakes his head. "We need to check the lake, see if we can find some."

I'm ninety-nine percent sure he's making the hairy-frog thing up, but I say, "Sounds great."

"No guinea pig in there," Lurena says when she comes back out. "I didn't even find droppings. Your dad keeps his study extremely neat and tidy."

"Yes, he is one excellent housekeeper. Any other ideas?"

"The garage."

She searches it top to bottom, including inside Dad's car and Fido's doghouse. Her dress gets some grease on it. As do her pets. They get to work licking it off.

When she finally admits failure, we go back to the house. Dad is in the kitchen, making us a snack. He sets homemade blueberry muffins and a pitcher of red iced tea on the table.

"It's hibiscus," he says. "Unsweetened."

"How very kind of you, Art," Lurena says.

Murphy and I look at each other. Is it really very kind to give kids unsweetened herbal tea?

Lurena puts her rodents in their portable cage, then goes to the bathroom to wash her hands. Dad glares at me till I do the same. Murphy comes with me.

"Still believe this the-more-the-merrier baloney?" I ask.

He laughs. "Absolutely!"

We go back to the table and both grab for the biggest muffin at the same time.

"Manners, Rufus," Dad says, and takes a sip of coffee. No unsweetened herbal tea for him. I bet he put sugar in his coffee when we were in the bathroom.

I sit back in my chair and let Murphy choose first. My dad and Lurena already picked theirs. I end up with the smallest one.

"I think Fido might be sick, and hiding," Lurena says as she pulls her muffin apart. "Rodents do that." She takes a bite. "Yum! *Fabulous* muffins, Art!"

"Thank you."

"But we've looked everywhere, Lurena," I say. "She must have gotten out of the house."

Dad bristles. "I'd like to know how she got out of Rufus's room."

"Sure she didn't slip by you when you checked on her?" I ask.

Stony Stare. No, Stony *Glare*.

"Did you hear about the hairy frogs at the lake?" Murphy asks him.

"The what?" As usual, Dad says the *h* before the *w*—*The hwat?*—but he really punches the *h* this time.

"I told you to stop," I say to Murphy out of the corner of my mouth.

"I thought Art might've heard about them." He looks at my dad. "They have claws, you know."

I kick him under the table with my boot. He keeps smiling.

"Are you referring to the so-called 'horror frog'?" Dad asks. "The species with the ring of dark hair around its waist? The frogs that break their own toes and use their bones for claws?"

My mouth drops open.

"Exactly!" Murphy says, smiling triumphantly.

"But at the lake?" Dad asks. "Isn't it an African species?"

"Do people keep them as pets, Art?" Lurena asks.

"I believe people actually capture them, cook them, and eat them," Dad says.

"You're right . . . they *do*," Murphy says.

"I wonder if they sell them at Exotique," Lurena says. "Maybe some escaped."

Murph snaps his fingers. "I think that's *precisely* what happened!"

Okay, so the hairy frogs with claws are real. Who knows, maybe there are even some at the lake. But don't we have more important things to discuss?

"Who cares?" I shout so loud that everyone jumps. "We're looking for *Fido*, not some freaky frogs! Can we stay focused, please?"

"Sorry," Murphy says, looking down at his lap.

Lurena turns to my dad. "Did you notice that Fido was bloated?"

"Not *bloated*! *Fat!*"

Stony Stare.

I groan and tell Lurena I'm sorry for yelling.

"I did notice," Dad says. "Rufus said it was likely due to Fido's consuming too much table food—which, incidentally, I have always discouraged. Rufus has been keeping Fido locked in her cage during dinner to prevent her from begging."

"And because he doesn't want her to act like a dog anymore," Lurena adds.

Dad looks at me, his eyebrows raised. "Is that why you've kept her in her cage, Rufus?"

I glare at Lurena.

"And is that why you locked her in your room all day?" Dad asks.

I don't want to answer. I don't want to be there anymore, with Dad looking at me that way, or with Lurena, the big traitor. I stand up and storm out of the room. Actually, I hobble out, which isn't nearly as satisfying.

20. Dad found me in the Dump.

I was lying on my back with my face buried in a stack of clothes. They smelled like detergent.

"Well, that was rude," he says.

"Nice opening," I answer into some balls of rolled-up socks.

"Sorry. So you're upset?"

"You think?" I shouldn't be sarcastic, but he really shouldn't say such dumb things.

"Do you want to sit up and talk to me about it, or shall we continue on like this?"

I almost say, *No, this is working for me*, but change my mind. I sit up and ask, "Did they leave?"

"No, they're waiting for you. I told them to give me a few minutes before coming up."

I fall back on my face. "I want to be alone."

"No time for Greta Garbo."

"Huh?"

"Reclusive old movie star. You don't like Fido anymore? You don't want her?"

"No."

"You don't like her?"

"I don't want her."

"Why don't you want her?"

I turn my head toward him. A ball of socks rolls off the bed and bounces silently on the carpet. "Do you see how everyone treats me at school now?"

"Yes. They like you."

"They don't like me. They aren't interested in me. It's Fido they're interested in. Fido, the guinea dog."

"So you're disappointed? Hurt?"

"No! I don't care what they think about me."

Do I?

"Then what do you care about?"

"They've been crowding around me all week, asking questions, talking to me. . . ."

"And that's bad because . . . ?"

"Because I don't want them to."

"You want to be left alone. Like Greta Garbo, the reclusive movie star."

"What's 'reclusive'?"

"Avoiding people. You don't like the attention?"

"I don't."

"Have you asked them to leave you alone?"

"You can't be alone at *school*!" What's with this guy? Was he never a student?

"You can't run up to your room and hide, that's for sure," he says.

"You can't run *any*where. There's nowhere to hide."

"So you figure the best solution to this problem is to give away your pet?"

"Please don't go all parental on me." I roll over and face the wall.

"Who better than I?" he asks, going all literal on me. Real sensitive parenting style he has. "I'm surprised you'd prefer giving away Fido to standing up for yourself, that's all. I thought Fido mattered to you."

I spin back around. "And what makes you think I can stand up for myself?"

"You're standing up to me. Well, from a supine position, of course . . ."

"Supine?"

"On your back."

I sit up. "But you're my dad, not a bunch of crazy kids."

"So just pretend you're talking to me when you talk to them."

"Or maybe I could pretend they're wearing underwear? That stuff is total cornball, Dad. Pretending! If it worked, I'd pretend I was Murphy. Or Batman."

His cheeks puff up, then his lips part and flutter as air escapes. It reminds me of what horses do.

"I wasn't trying to be funny," I say.

"Sorry." He covers his mouth with his hand. "I guess your worries are over now anyway. It would seem Fido divined your feelings about her and flew the coop."

"What?"

"Fido felt unwanted and ran away."

"But *how*?"

There's a knock.

"Ready for us yet?" Lurena asks through the door.

Before I can say no, Dad lets her in. Murphy steps in behind her.

"You okay, Roof?" he asks.

I shrug. How embarrassing is it that I screamed and ran to my room in front of him? About a twelve on a scale of one to ten.

"Where did the clothes come from?" Lurena asks, walking over and picking up the ball of socks from the floor.

The nerve! I tear it out of her hands. She looks shocked, like she never dreamed I wouldn't want her pawing my clothes.

"It's just that they weren't here when we searched your room before," she says.

"They weren't?"

I look down at the socks I'm holding. I look at my dad. I think he's having the same thought I'm having, because, for the third time since he came in here, he tells me he's sorry.

21. The socks gave him away.

"Did you put clean clothes on my bed yesterday, too—the day Fido disappeared?" I ask Dad.

"Forgive me. I washed your clothes and delivered them to your room. And pity me that my hard work goes unnoticed."

Lurena and Murphy are looking at us with confused expressions. So I explain.

"Fido slipped out right under his nose. His arms were full of clothes when he came in. He couldn't look down."

"Oh!" they say together.

"I wasn't holding the clothes in my arms. I had them in a basket."

"You still wouldn't have been able to look down," I say.

"She didn't get by me. She was curled up on the bed and didn't move when I emptied the basket of your freshly laundered clothes and set them on the bed next to her. She scooted up to them and closed her eyes."

"Was she there when you left?" Lurena asks.

My dad cocks his head. "I'm not sure." He scratches his chin. He's trying to remember. "She had to be. She didn't have time to . . ." His voice trails off.

"She's pretty fast," Murphy says.

"*Really* fast," I say.

"I set the basket down and noticed something on the floor. It was gum. Used gum." He flicks me a look. "I knelt down to get it, but couldn't extricate it from the carpet, so I made a mental note that later I should both reprimand my son and give him some vinegar and a brush with which to remove the foul substance."

"And then you left?" Lurena asks.

"Yes, I lifted the basket and happily exited this wretched place." He glances around the room. "Oh my, you *cleaned* it."

I ignore his drama. "And you didn't check to see that Fido was still on the bed?"

He stiffens up. His jaw tightens. "She did not run by me. I guarantee it. I would have seen her."

"She probably jumped into the basket," Lurena says. "You carried her out, Art."

"She escaped by hiding in the laundry, like in a prison break movie!" Murphy says.

Dad shrugs. "I suppose it's possible. . . ."

"It doesn't matter," I say. "The question is, what do we do now? How do we find her?"

"I thought you didn't want a guinea dog anymore," Lurena says.

I don't like her snooty tone, or the question. I regret saying I didn't want Fido. I do want her. I just don't want everyone else to want her. I wish I weren't the only kid in the world who owned a guinea dog. I wish there were more like her.

Hey, wait a minute. More like her? *More like her!*

"I get it!" I practically shout. "I get why she's fat, why she's hiding! I get it! I *get* it!"

22. Dogs don't build nests.

Not like birds do, anyway. Or wasps. But they do like a quiet, undisturbed place to deliver their pups.

I remember Murphy's mom moved Buddy's dog bed into the laundry room when Buddy was going to have puppies. She had two boys and a girl. One of the boys was stillborn. They found homes for the other two. Not my home, of course. Dad wouldn't allow it.

According to Lurena, guinea pigs don't build nests, either. They do like quiet, undisturbed places to deliver their babies, though, like dogs. And Fido is a guinea pig that acts like a dog.

And she is fat.

"If she's pregnant, she probably didn't run away," Lurena says after I tell her my theory.

"But we looked everywhere here," I say.

"How did she get pregnant?" Murphy asks.

We all look at him. There's an awkward moment of silence. Then he adds, "You know what I mean."

"Was it one of your pets, Lurena?" Dad asks. "You've brought them here often enough."

"China C. and Sharmet are both female," she says.

"How can you tell?" he asks.

"The way you always do with mammals."

There's another awkward silence.

Murphy breaks it. "It can't be Buddy, can it? I mean, Fido really acts like a dog. . . ."

"Buddy's female, too!" Lurena says.

Murphy laughs. "Oh, right!"

"Mars?" I ask. I sincerely hope not.

"No, no," Lurena says. "You haven't had Fido long enough for her to . . ." Gratefully, she let that hang there. "She must have been pregnant when you got her."

"*If* she's pregnant," Dad says.

I can tell he's hoping she isn't. He's okay with Fido, but I doubt he wants more like her.

I hope she's pregnant. It's sure better than her running away because I was mean to her.

"How many babies can a guinea pig have?" I ask Lurena.

"As many as six, but it's usually three or four."

"Three or four!" Dad gasps.

"On average. But sometimes a sow has only two. Or even just one."

"A 'sow'?" Murphy says.

"A female guinea pig is called a sow." Lurena says this as if everyone should already know it.

"Like a pig," Dad says.

"What do they call the babies?" I ask.

"'Piglets'?" Murphy asks. "'Puplets'?"

"Some people say 'puppy' or 'pup,'" Lurena says. "Some say 'piglet.' It's controversial."

"In this particular case," Dad says, a bit miserably, "I think we're dealing with pups."

"So how do we find her?" I ask. "Where would she be?"

"She could be anywhere," Lurena says, looking at me seriously, as if she's trying to teach me something. "But I don't think she wants to be found."

23. Piñatas are twisted.

It doesn't matter what shape they are.

For my fourth birthday party, my mom bought a piñata that looked like Winnie the Pooh. I guess I was into Pooh then. I don't remember. Anyway, my mom gave me a stick and told me to beat Pooh with it. First his leg came off, then his other leg, then an arm, then an ear. . . . It took forever to break him open because blindfolded little kids are bad at hitting things with sticks, but finally my friends and I were able to bust lovable Pooh Bear to bits. Then we all dove to the ground and scrambled for the candy that fell out of his belly. We shoved, trampled, elbowed, and growled like starving, savage beasts, because we wanted more candy than our friends.

That's what I mean by twisted.

For my ninth birthday, my mom bought one in the shape of a rottweiler. She probably thought it might make me feel better about not being allowed to have a real one. It didn't. My friends and I bashed the rottweiler to bits, too.

"I'm too old for piñatas," I say to my mom that night at dinner.

We're sitting at the table, discussing my party. I don't want a party. I'm sick of crowds. But Mom has her mind set on it.

"You like piñatas, don't you?" she asks with a pout.

"Sure." I don't want to hurt her feelings. But I realize that if I'd told her the truth earlier, I wouldn't have had to put up with piñatas all these years.

Maybe that's true about a lot of things. Maybe saying I don't like something would save me from putting up with a lot of stuff I don't like. Like getting mobbed at school. Or eating my dad's sauerkraut, which I'm doing to be polite. It's ruining a perfectly good turkey dog. (Actually, turkey dogs can never be perfect. Hot dogs, sure, but not turkey dogs.)

"What would you like instead?" Mom asks.

I'd like no party.

I should tell her.

I don't want to hurt her feelings. She wants me to want a party.

I really don't want one.

I really should tell her.

I should.

I really should.

I'm going to tell her.

She's going to be crushed.

I close my eyes.

"I don't want a party at all."

"You . . . don't?"

I can't tell from her expression if she's hurt or just shocked. This is because my eyes are still closed.

I open them. I swallow. Hard.

"No, I don't."

My dad smiles at me. I wonder why. Is he proud of me? Or doesn't he like parties, either?

"Then no party," he says, turning his smile

to my mom, where it becomes softer, as if to comfort her. "What should we do instead?"

I jump in here. "Maybe I could invite Murphy over and we could go to the new skate park in Irondale—"

"Anything that doesn't require two healthy feet?" Dad interrupts, still smiling.

"How about *four* healthy feet?" I give him a knowing look, a how-about-a-dog-for-my-birthday look. It's a risk, but he has been really nice since he realized he probably let Fido out of my room.

The niceness vanishes, leaving behind the Stony Stare. *But*, he doesn't say no immediately, like usual. Is he actually considering it?

Maybe Fido showed him a pet isn't such a bad thing. That a *dog* isn't such a bad thing. Fido's not a dog, but she did a pretty good impression of one. Now that she's gone—if she is gone—maybe Dad is finally ready to get a real dog.

And it's when I think these words that we hear a faint, distant *woof*!

We leap to our feet.

24. Tiny turkeys.

That's what we hear. Tiny *gobble-gobble-gobble* sounds. Or maybe the sound of someone rubbing tiny balloons. It's a rubbery sound. But tiny. A tiny, rubber-turkey sound.

It's mixed with Fido's muted, distant barking, and leads us down to the basement, to the laundry room. I searched here before. She must have found a great hiding spot and stayed really quiet. And I must have searched before the pups were born.

We're all convinced that the tiny, rubber-turkey sound is coming from guinea pig pups, even though none of us has ever heard a guinea pig pup before. What else could it be? Someone making balloon animals in our dark basement?

Eww! I just creeped myself out! I really hope that's not what's making the sound!

The sounds are coming from a stack of cardboard boxes. On the boxes are words written in my dad's careful cursive: OLD PHOTOS, RAQUEL'S JOURNALS, ART'S COLLEGE NOTEBOOKS, WINTER CLOTHES, BABY CLOTHES. We didn't move them before when we searched because they were so big and heavy. If we couldn't move them, how could Fido move them?

When we slide the boxes out from the wall, we discover a hole in one of them. Obviously, Fido had squeezed behind it and gnawed her way into the box. BABY CLOTHES is written on it.

I wonder for a second if Mom is going to be upset about this, but instead she squeals, "She had her babies in your *baby* clothes! Isn't that sweet?"

It isn't sweet, actually. It's sour. Like a rodent cage that hasn't been cleaned for a while. I notice little red dots on the clothes. Blood? If it is, I hope bleeding is normal when guinea pigs give birth.

Fido's lying on her side on a blue baby

blanket. She lifts her head when she sees us peeking into the hole. She looks right at me. Her eyes seem dull and wet. Is she sad? Tired? Sick?

"Fido?" I say. "You okay? Come, girl! Come!"

She doesn't.

"She's busy with her babies," Mom says.

"Where are they?" I ask. It's hard to see inside the box. It's really dark in this corner of the basement, even with the lights on.

"Behind her?" Dad suggests. "I hope there aren't a lot of them."

"We know, Art," Mom says, patting his arm. "You've said so a dozen times."

"What do we do?" I ask. "Should we carry the box up to my room? I'm sure she needs food and water."

"I'm sure you're right," Mom says. "But maybe we should call Lurena. She's the expert on these things."

"Do we have to?"

I've seen and heard an awful lot of Lurena lately.

Then again, she did help me look for

Fido. She has been a kind of an okay friend.

"I guess we can call her," I say. "Maybe she can tell us about the bloodstains. Though I know she'll run right over when she hears what we found."

"It's seven thirty on a school night," Dad says.

True.

I call her. She picks up on the first ring.

"Did you find her? How many babies? Can I have a couple? I prefer the females, of course."

"Down, girl," I say, and fill her in on the situation.

She says the blood is normal, and it's okay to carry the box up to my room, but to do it carefully.

"Really? Because I was thinking I'd just stand at the bottom of the stairs and chuck it."

I'm being sarcastic, but actually, my throwing it might be safer than carrying it upstairs with this medical boot.

"Have your mom carry it up. You have that boot, remember?"

She's kind of psychic. Also, kind of psycho.

"I wish I could come over and help. I'm sure my parents won't let me."

Phew. "We can handle it."

"Be sure to give her some food and water right away. And not just meat, Rufus. Give her some fresh grass. When she comes out of the box to get it, you can count the babies. Oh, I hope she had a lot of them!"

"That's exactly how my dad *doesn't* feel."

"I get two sows, okay?"

It occurs to me that the babies might become a problem. Every kid in town is going to want one. Murphy wants one. Lurena expects two. Dmitri will want all of them.

I sure hope Fido had a lot of pups.

25. One.

That's how many we find in the box after Fido comes out to eat and drink. One guinea pup.

Dad is so relieved.

The pup looks a lot like Fido, only smaller. Quite a bit smaller. Fido looks huge next to it, in fact. The pup is more yellow than orange, but it does have its mom's spiky white mohawk. It's also feisty like its mom. It scurries around the nest, stopping occasionally to rise up on its hind legs and look around, then goes back to its scurrying. It's making that rubbery, gobbly sound we heard, nonstop.

I have to say "it," by the way, until it grows bigger and Lurena can check to see if it's a sow or a boar.

I notice Fido looks skinnier as she nibbles at the leftover salmon and fresh grass I bring her. She's also looks tired. Too tired to come when I call her. At least I hope that's why she won't come. I hope that she's not mad at me, that she's forgiven me.

But I don't push. She's been through quite an ordeal. That's what my mom says, anyway, and she should know. She must have gone through quite an ordeal when I was born. Dad is always saying what a gigantic baby I was, as if I had anything to do with it. It's not like I was pigging out on pizza and ice cream in there.

I'm glad I'll never have to go through the kind of ordeal Mom and Fido did.

After Fido finishes her dinner, she waddles back into the box to her baby.

"Couldn't you just *die*?" Mom asks in a squeaky voice. "It is so cute, I could just *die*!"

Again, does cuteness kill? Am I missing something?

"I'm just glad there's only one of them," Dad says. "We *are* certain there's only one, aren't we? We *have* thoroughly searched the box for others, yes?"

"There's only one," I say, glad I can make him glad.

I did thoroughly search the box, pulling out little pairs of pajamas with pictures of rockets or dinosaurs or bulldozers on them, and a tiny red baseball cap with an *R* on the front (for my name, I assume), and a miniature black T-shirt with white letters reading BABY TALK STRICTLY FORBIDDEN. My guess is Dad bought that one. I also found a pair of baby cowboy boots, and a pair of baby overalls. I didn't find any extra baby guinea dogs.

Which was disappointing, actually. If there had been more, and they ended up acting like their mom, there would be lots of guinea dogs to go around. That would mean more satisfied classmates, who would leave me alone.

"What are we going to do with it?" Dad asks. His face says he doesn't want to keep it. One guinea pig is his limit.

"Oh, let's not think about that now," Mom

says. "She'll need her mother for weeks, I'm sure. That will give us plenty of time to decide."

It's Fido's turn to be laid up awhile, and my turn to take care of her, like she did for me. I like the thought of that.

"Let's leave them alone then and get downstairs and clean up the kitchen," Dad says.

Mom must see my disappointment, because she says, "Art, how about we let Rufus stay here with the guinea pigs? I know he's excited to see Fido again, not to mention her adorable little baby. We can do the dishes."

Yay, Mom!

Dad doesn't like it, but he lets me stay. The two of them head downstairs.

I pull my blankets and pillow down from my bed and make a little nest for myself next to the box. I watch Fido through the hole, nursing her baby. She lies on her side as the pup burrows happily into her belly.

"I missed you," I say quietly. "I'm sorry about the way I treated you. It was stupid . . . and selfish. I want you to be exactly the way you are. Okay?"

She doesn't raise her head or look at me. My heart sinks. I guess she's still upset at me.

Then I notice her rear end wagging ever so slightly. She's wagging her nonexistent tail.

I think we're good.

26. "No."

It's a short word, easy to say, except when it isn't. Sometimes it's the hardest word in the world to say. But I promised myself I'd say it.

"Can I come to your house and see the guinea dog?"

"No."

"Can you take a picture of me with your guinea dog?"

"No."

"Will you sell me your guinea dog?"

"No."

"Can I have your new baby guinea dog?"

This is Lurena. She promised not to tell anyone about the pup. Only she, Murphy, my parents, and I know about it, and that's how

I want it to stay. But her promise doesn't stop her from asking this question whenever no one can hear her.

"No," I say.

We're walking home. Actually, I'm walking home. She's following me home. Uninvited.

I honestly don't know what I should do with Fido's pup. I know Dad won't let me keep it. I wish Fido would tell me somehow. I doubt a mother ever wants to give up her baby.

For the first time I think about Fido having a mother. She had to have one, of course. Everybody has to. I wonder if Fido thinks about her. Misses her. I would.

"My mom says no to a ground squirrel," Lurena says. "She says they're not tame enough and that they have sharp teeth."

"Maybe they're right."

"Don't be ridiculous. Lots of pets have sharp teeth. Dogs. Cats. Snakes. And lots of people have ground squirrels for pets these days. They're totally safe. Safer than a lot of other pets, that's for sure. It's not like I want a dog.

Did you know dogs hurt more people than any other mammal?"

"Not *all* dogs."

"But my mom says no ground squirrel, and no means no. That's what she always says anyway."

"She's right. No does mean no."

"I don't think one should take no for an answer from someone who's being unreasonable, do you?"

"No." I've never taken Dad's noes about a dog seriously. He's being totally unreasonable.

"So what do you say? The guinea pup would be an excellent substitute. . . ."

"I don't want to talk about it right now, okay?"

"Okay, okay. Goodness, what a grouch! Can I at least come in and visit it?"

We've arrived at my house. She's talked the whole way.

"I guess," I say. I'm still not as good at saying no as I want to be.

We go in.

"Dad! I'm home," I call.

He doesn't answer. Must be in the middle of a sentence. That's what he tells me: *Can't talk. I'm in the middle of a sentence.*

We walk into the kitchen. Mom's there. And Murphy. And Dmitri.

"Surprise!" they say.

27. It's not my birthday.

Maybe that's part of the surprise?

What isn't surprising is that Mom forgot I didn't want a party. Or ignored that I didn't. Or maybe she didn't hear me. I really do think she needs her hearing tested.

She prances over and hugs me.

"Oh, happy birthday, my big little boy!"

I peek over my shoulder and see Lurena smiling, Murphy winking, and Dmitri smirking with delight. Great.

I cannot believe Mom invited Dmitri. Talk about clueless. And Lurena helped with the guest list. This is what happens when these two put their heads together.

"It's tomorrow, Mom. My birthday's tomorrow."

"What's all the noise?" Dad asks, stepping into the room, and looking as surprised as I am. "I'm right in the middle of a sentence."

So this was all Mom's idea. It's like when she bought Fido. She makes decisions involving all of us, and we find out about it later.

"It's just a little birthday gathering," she says, and smiles at me. "It's not a party."

So I guess she did hear me.

She just didn't listen.

"I do have a cake," she says, finally releasing me from the hug. "But we don't have to sing if you don't want us to."

"I don't want you to."

She wilts a little, but quickly perks back up. "Your friends are staying for dinner. We'll have a pizza par . . . a pizza *part* of the gathering later on."

"Nice save."

I notice several wrapped presents sitting on the table. Maybe this isn't so bad after all.

"Where's Fido?" Dmitri asks.

No, it's bad.

Murphy and Lurena look away. They know

I don't want Dmitri to know about the pup. The problem is my parents, as it so often is. They could easily give it away. Especially my mom.

"I'm sure she's resting, Dmitri," she says.

"Why?" he asks.

Murphy steps in, wraps his arm around Dmitri's shoulders, and steers him away from my bigmouth mother.

"Why do you think?" he asks. "Roof's dad took her on a run today. Six miles. Say, have you heard about the new phone that takes X-rays?"

He leads Dmitri toward the living room, and Dmitri goes happily. Cool electronic devices and Murphy Molloy are two of his favorite things.

"I took Fido on a six-mile run?" Dad asks. "I don't run."

It's true. He doesn't.

"I don't want Dmitri to know about the pup," I whisper.

Normally, Dad frowns on deceit. That's how he puts it: *I frown on deceit.* But this time he seems down with it.

"I understand," he says.

I look at Mom.

She nods. "Fine. But I think open communication is always the best—"

"Mom," I interrupt, "Dmitri is not my friend. He's mean to me pretty much all the time. The only reason he comes over is because he wants Fido."

"Oh," Mom says, looking a bit stunned.

"If he finds out about the pup, he'll want it, and when I say no, he'll tell everyone at school about it, and everyone will want one, and everyone will drive me nuts, and I'll be ever so sad. I may even have to run away from home. Like, forever."

"Okay, I get it," she says. "Try to calm down, Rufus."

I guess I am a little worked up. I have part of her sleeve gripped in my fist.

"Sorry," I say, releasing it.

"It should be easy enough to keep it a secret from him," Lurena says. "All you have to do is keep him out of your room."

"But he wants to see Fido."

"We'll stick to our story about the run," Dad says.

"As if you could run six miles!" Mom laughs.

For once, it's not me who gets the Stony Stare.

"Why don't you order the pizza, darling?" Mom says in reply.

Dad nods and goes to the phone.

"Rufus, go out back and tell the boys it's cake time," Mom says.

"Before the pizza?" Lurena asks.

"Well, it's too early for dinner, so I thought we'd have the cake first. I didn't think you guys would mind."

I didn't mind.

"I'm sure it's fine," I say. "I'll go tell them."

"Lurena, will you help me carry the cake and dishes out?" Mom asks. "Rufus can't with the boot and all. Besides, it's his birthday."

"It will be my pleasure," Lurena says. "But may I go up and peek at the baby a minute first?"

"No," I say.

"Oh, *please*. I'm dying to see it."

"So die already. It's too risky."

"Just for a second? Murphy will keep Dmitri amused."

"A second can't hurt," Mom says.

"Thanks, Raquel," Lurena says.

I don't like it when these two get together.

"Okay, one second," I say. "I mean it, Lurena. *One.* Not five. Not two. And don't let Dmitri see you going up."

"Thanks!" she says, and flies up the stairs.

"She wants the pup, too, you know," I say to my mom.

She smiles. "I'm sure she'd take good care of her."

So that's who my mom thinks should get the pup.

I wonder who I think should.

28. Singing is for the birds.

I don't like doing it or having it done to me.

I stare at the little flickering flames until the singing is over. I don't make a wish. I never do. I just close my eyes and pretend to. A long time ago I wished no one would ever sing "Happy Birthday" to me again, so obviously wishing on candles doesn't work. I blow them out, and everyone applauds, like blowing out birthday candles is some great achievement.

Mom lifts them out of the frosting while they're still smoking, licks each one, then cuts the cake. It's my favorite: chocolate with chocolate frosting. She also got my favorite ice cream: chocolate chunk with cookie dough. Except for the singing, and the worrying about Dmitri, I'm really enjoying my birthday gathering.

We finish our cake in about twenty seconds, then I start opening my presents. Lurena's is a bike bell. It's an old-fashioned one, the kind that looks like half of a chrome yo-yo laid on its side, only this one has a orange guinea pig face painted on it. Yes, it has a white mohawk.

"I painted it myself," she says proudly, though no one asked.

"It's beautiful!" Mom gushes.

I'm not going to put it on my bike. It's a little girly. And you don't put bells on a BMX. That's ridiculous. But it probably did take time and effort to buy and to paint the guinea pig on it, so I say thanks. It's the polite thing to do.

Murphy gives me a striped tail on a stick, which is a weird gift. I hope it's not a real tail from a real animal.

"It's a coatimundi tail," Murphy says. "A real one."

"What's a coatimundi?" Dmitri asks.

"Why not look it up on your phone?" I say.

He shrugs, but takes out his phone, asks

how to spell it, and starts thumb-typing. If a coatimundi is a real animal, I want to see it, so I lean over to look.

"Back off," he says.

"Hey, I'm the birthday boy."

"Your birthday is tomorrow."

"This one's from Dmitri," Mom interrupts, and hands me a white plastic grocery bag with a knowing look. "He said he didn't have time to wrap it."

Dmitri doesn't even look up from his phone.

Inside the bag is a digital speedometer. It's not in a box. It's not in a package. It's not new. It's been used. Still, it's pretty cool.

"Thanks," I say.

"Here it is," he says. "It looks like a skinny raccoon with a long tail."

He's right. It does.

"Yeah, except coatimundis are venomous," Murphy says.

"Like ducks?" I ask.

He ignores this. "It's way cooler to bike down the street with the tail of a venomous coatimundi fluttering behind you than with the tail of some ordinary, garbage-eating raccoon, like most people do."

"Is that what most people do?" Lurena asks.

Suddenly, it hits me what's going on.

Bell.

Speedometer.

Tail on a stick for my wheel.

I look up at my mom, and she's grinning ear to ear. I think she's actually grinning wider than that. Dad's nodding at me. Murphy and Lurena start laughing out loud.

Guess who got a new bike for his birthday!

"It's in the garage," Dad says.

I run as fast as a kid in a medical boot can.

It's a single-speed road bike, green as mint ice cream, with bullhorn handlebars wrapped in brown tape, and skinny tires with white rims. It's totally different from my BMX, which is perfect. I've been dropping hints to my parents that I wanted a road bike for months. I told them I needed one because riding a BMX on the street is dangerous, but the real reason is speed. I want to go faster.

I rush over to the bike and lift it with one

hand. It's light as a feather. It's also too tall for me, which is how it's supposed to be.

I can't believe it's mine. I want to jump on it and take off on a long ride. And I want Fido running alongside me. And Murphy and Buddy, too.

"It's a shame you can't ride it," Mom says with a long face. "We bought it before you broke your foot."

And before we knew Fido was pregnant. Shoot. She can't run alongside my bike.

"It's okay," I lie. "Thanks. It's glorious."

"Nice word choice," she says, and hugs me. I don't groan or sigh. That's how glorious the bike is.

"Thanks, Dad," I gasp over her shoulder.

"I'm sorry it's not a dog," he says.

"I'll trade you my dog for Fido," Dmitri says.

Before my dad can say, "No way," I say, "No, thanks." I wouldn't want Mars even if Dad said yes. And I won't ever trade Fido, for anything.

Dmitri stuffs his phone in his pocket and moves toward my bike. "Since you can't ride it, how about I take it for a spin?"

I'd like to be polite and share and all, but the guy can't take my bike for its first spin.

This is an excellent opportunity for me to try out a good, strong no.

Do I chicken out this time?

"No," I say. "Sorry, but I want to be the first to ride it."

"But you *can't. . . .*"

"Oh, he can ride it easy," Murphy says. "I've seen him do it."

My mom's mouth falls open.

So does mine. Why is he squealing on me?

"I'll get the coatimundi tail," he says, and bolts.

"Wait. I'll get the speedometer!" Dmitri yells, and runs after him.

"Get the bike bell, too!" Lurena yells.

When the gifts are all attached, I climb aboard my new bike, which isn't easy. It's tall for one thing. For another, one of my feet is wearing Frankenstein's boot. I can't swing it over the bike or put my weight on it.

"Art? Is this okay?" Mom asks in a worried voice.

I stop grappling with the bike and look at Dad. *Come on, Art,* I think. *Back me up here. For once.*

"It's fine," he says.

"Yes!" I say. Murph hoists me up, and I pedal away.

29. The new bike is fast as lightning, if lightning goes sixteen miles an hour.

That's how fast I'm going, according to my new (Dmitri's old) speedometer. Imagine how fast it'll go when I'm not wearing the boot.

I glance over my shoulder to see the long coatimundi tail streaming behind me. I wonder if it's real. Nah. Coatimundis may be real, but that is definitely a fake coatimundi tail.

"Coati*mundi*!" I yell, pumping my fist in the air. I ring the Fido bell. I feel all my worries disappear.

What did I have to complain about anyway? So I broke my foot. So some kids wanted my pet guinea pig. So I was being pestered by a weird girl and a mean guy. So my guinea pig had a baby and I couldn't decide who to give it to. So what?

What's more important right now is that I have the coolest guinea pig in the world—one that everyone wants—that this is my last day being ten, that I'm riding the best bike ever built. The foot will heal, the boot will come off, Fido will be herself again. It'll just take a little time. Not much at all, really.

When I turn the corner back onto our cul-de-sac, everyone starts running at me, everyone being Murphy, Lurena, Dmitri, Mom, and even Dad. Yeah, Art is running. Out in front is Fido, her tongue flapping in the wind.

"Ruff!" she says.

"Hey, girl!" I answer, slowing down so I don't accidentally run her over. "How you doing? Feeling okay? You must! Look at you—you're running! Look at *me*—I'm riding my new bike! Sweet, eh? Want to take a lap around the block with me?"

Yeah, I'm talking to her like she's a person. Or a dog. So what?

"Rufus!" Mom and Lurena yell at the same time.

They're upset. I should have realized something was wrong, that they weren't just running up to meet me. I mean, why would Dad be running if he didn't have to?

Are they trying to catch Fido? Maybe she shouldn't be running so soon after giving birth.

I squeeze the brakes. They're grabbier than my BMX's. My back tire freezes and I go into a skid. The bike starts sliding out from under me. I put my foot down, but I'm so high up that I can't reach the ground. I lose control. My foot hits the pavement first—the booted foot, the bad one—and gives. Twists. Hurts. My glorious new bike and I spill onto the street. The guinea pig bell rings.

"RUFUS!" Mom shrieks.

Fido reaches me first. She bites onto my shirtsleeve and tugs, like she's trying to pick me up.

"Hold on," I say, as I try to push my bike off me. It doesn't feel so light when it's on you.

Fido keeps tugging and whimpering as the others catch up.

"Take it easy," I tell her. "I'm a cripple, remember?"

That's when I notice she's not looking at me. She's looking up over my head. She's not trying to help me up. She wants me to see something.

"What is it, girl?" I ask, then look up—directly into the sun. I flinch.

"It's the pup!" Lurena says, appearing over me, pointing to the sky. "Up there!"

"The pup is up?" I ask, sounding like Dr. Seuss: *Up is the pup? The pup is UP!*

My mom lifts the bike and helps me to my feet. My bad foot aches. Did I rebreak it? Will I have to stay in bed, miss school, hang out with Fido and the pup . . . ?

Wait a minute. That doesn't sound so bad.

"Goodness!" Mom says, dusting me off. "You okay, sweetie?"

"Never mind that. How's my new bike? It's not scratched, is it?"

Lurena elbows me. Hard. She sure has bony

elbows. "Will you *look* already? Up there! On the wire! Look!"

"Take it easy. Sheesh. I'm looking."

All I see are trees and the sky above them. And the sun. I shield my eyes. I see the wire. It's a power line, or a phone line maybe. Or is it a cable? I don't know my wires. I see a small creature walking along the wire like it's a tightrope. A squirrel, probably.

No.

Not a squirrel.

Not unless it's a squirrel with a white mohawk.

30. Proof my life is weirder than weird.

- My dad doesn't like dogs.
- My mom thinks a guinea pig is a good substitute for a dog.
- My dog is a guinea pig.
- A girl is my friend.
- My friend thinks a squirrel is a great pet.
- My guinea dog's baby is a squirrel.
- My guinea dog's baby is a trapeze artist.

"Isn't it stupendous!" Lurena squeals as we watch the pup run down a tree trunk toward her whining mother, Fido, on the ground. "You wanted a dog, and I wanted a ground squirrel, and you got a guinea pig that acts like a dog, and she gave birth to a guinea pup that acts like a squirrel! Stupendous!"

"Yeah," I say.

It is pretty stupendous. Hard to believe, actually. And kind of creepy. It's another one of Murphy's crazy stories come true. There really are hairy, clawed horror frogs, and coatimundis. The world we live in is filled with weird creatures.

Lurena, for example.

"I'm going to name her Queen Girlisaur!" she says.

"Isn't that kind of overkill? You know, *queen* and *girly* in the same name? A girly queen is sort of . . . what do you call it . . . ?"

"Redundant?" Dad pitches in.

"I think it's precious," Mom says.

Exactly. And who wants that?

"What if it isn't a girl?" Murphy asks.

Lurena makes a deep-in-thought face, then says, "I'll come up with a nickname."

"Queenie?" Mom suggests. "Or how about Girlie?"

"How about Rocky?" Murph says.

"Like the boxer?" Dmitri asks.

Murph laughs. "No! The flying squirrel!"

"Hey, wait a minute," I interrupt. "Who says you get the pup?"

"Yeah!" Dmitri huffs. "Why should she get it? She's already got two rodents. I should get it."

"You have pets, too," Lurena says. "A guinea pig and the black puffball of death."

She must have heard me call Mars that.

"Look, Roof, I want it," Dmitri says with great seriousness. "Since you won't help me get a guinea dog, or train my guinea pig to act like one, the least you could do is give me the guinea pig baby that acts like a squirrel. I'll pay you. How much?"

Lurena ignores him and sits down in the grass by the guinea pigs. The pup has found a nut somewhere and is holding it in her paws and gnawing it, squirrel-style. The only thing missing is the long bushy tail.

"She's eating solid food already," Mom says.

"Yes," Lurena says. "Guinea pig pups often eat solid food right away. But they keep on nursing, too."

It does seem pretty obvious that the pup is perfect for Lurena, and vice versa. And I don't care how much money Dmitri offers me, he's not getting her. He's mean. Period.

But how will I explain to everyone at school that I gave the second coolest guinea pig ever to a girl? Especially an annoying, dorky, pushy girl like Lurena. A girl who barges into your house without being invited. A girl who barges into your *life* without being invited, and won't leave. A girl who wears clothes about three hundreds years out of style. A girl who carries rodents around in her bike basket.

It won't matter how I explain it.

So I won't. Who says I have to? Just because people want something from me doesn't mean I have to give it to them.

"No," I say to Dmitri. "Lurena gets the pup."

Lurena smiles. Murphy does, too. He gets why I'm making this decision.

Dmitri does not smile.

"No?" he repeats, shocked. And angry. "What do you mean 'No'?"

"Don't you know what no means, Dmitri?"

Lurena asks teasingly. "Why, it means no."

Dmitri snarls at her like a wild animal. A wolverine, maybe. Or Mars. Then he turns back to me.

"Look, I said I'd *pay* you for her. I'll *buy* her from you. Name your price. I can afford it."

He means his dad can afford it.

Then he makes an offer. A handsome one.

I say nothing. I said no, and I meant it.

He makes more offers.

I keep saying nothing. No was my final word on the subject. Saying it was not as awful as I thought it would be. It actually felt pretty good, like when you find you can lift something you thought was too heavy for you.

I wish I'd said it all week when everyone was getting in my face, making demands, prying into my personal business. From now on I'm not going to not say it when I want to say it. I'll start tomorrow, at school.

The pizza delivery guy arrives, breaking the tension. We all head back to the house, to the picnic table in the backyard. Dad ordered my favorite pizza: sausage with extra sausage. It's

Fido's favorite, too. She begs, and I feed her a sausage circle. Half of it hangs out of her mouth.

"I guess it wasn't table scraps that made her fat after all," Dad says.

"Guess not," I say.

"Still, you shouldn't feed her people food," Lurena says. "Especially meat. Guinea pigs are vegetarian."

Right then Queenie waddles up to her mom and licks her snout.

"No!" Lurena says. "Don't eat that, Queen Girlisaur! Don't! Oh, Rufus! Do you see what you've done?"

But Queen Girlisaur doesn't eat the sausage. She wants to nurse.

For a while nobody talks. We just scarf down the pizza, which is one of the greatest inventions of all time.

Lurena removed all the sausage from her slice, by the way. She's vegetarian, too. This doesn't ruin it—cheese pizza is still better than almost every other food—but it does bring its stupendousness down a couple notches.

As we eat, I think about how Lurena will be taking the pup home with her. Not right away, of course. Not till Queenie's weaned. I'm sure Lurena will bring her back a lot to visit her mom. Who knows, maybe sometimes I'll even bring Fido over to her house. . . .

No. I won't be doing that.

It hits me that Lurena adopting the pup makes us sort of related. The more I think about this, I realize being related will be better than being friends. It's a connection based on our pets. We'll be like family, and no one gets to choose their family. We all just get who we get. It's not strange for a boy to have to spend time with a girl in his family—a sister, or a girl cousin—even if he totally despises her. I don't despise the adoptive mother of my guinea pig's baby. But I don't exactly like her, either. There have been times when I haven't minded her so much. When she stood up for me, for example. Though I also dislike her when she does that.

It's complicated.

31. I'm too young to be a grandpa.

Murphy elbows me, and says it again.

"Come on, Grandpa! Let's Frizz it up! Fido, too!"

Fido hears her name, and gets up on her feet, ready to play.

"She just had a baby," I say. "She can't jump."

"I'll throw low."

"What about my foot?"

It still hurts, though I didn't break it again. I can't decide if that's a good thing or not.

"My throws will be strikes. You won't even have to move."

"I want to Frizz it up, too," Dmitri says, running away backward. "Frizz me a strike, Murph!"

"Did I just hear a car pull into the driveway?" Dad interrupts. "Your ride home, Dmitri, perhaps?"

Am I wrong or does Dad sound happy about this?

A horn honks.

"Aw, man," Dmitri says. He glares at me. "I got to go. Look, dude. I want that guinea pig baby. You can't give it to that freak. Understand?"

I say nothing. I've already given him my answer.

The horn honks again, longer and louder this time.

"I want it!" he says over his shoulder.

I have no further comment.

He's gone. We hear the car door open and close, then the car drives away.

"He didn't even say thank you," Lurena says. "Or good-bye." She shakes her head. "I don't care for that boy."

"I'm sure he has good points," Mom says, but not very convincingly. Which says a lot about Dmitri. Mom finds good points in everyone. In every*thing*.

Murphy laughs. "Sometimes I guess it's the less the merrier!"

Wow. He's really growing up.

"You're going to get more attention once Dmitri tells everyone about the guinea squirrel, you know," he says.

I shrug. He's right, but I don't care. Right now I don't, anyway. And when they come at me at school, I'll try real hard not to care then, either. I don't have to give anyone anything I don't want to. Including *my* attention.

"It's Frizz time!" Murph says.

He runs away from the table with the Frisbee. I hobble and wince. He floats me a perfect strike: between my knees and my chest and within arm's reach. I catch it.

"I want in!" Lurena says, skipping out onto the grass. "Throw it here, Rufus!"

Must she ruin everything?

I look at Murph. He smiles. I look at Mom. She's smiling. I look at Dad. Stony Stare.

I sigh and throw the disc to Lurena. Hard, and with plenty of spin. Let's see her catch *that*.

The throw is pretty high, and hooks sharply.

Lurena chases after it, yelling, "I got it! I got it!"

But she doesn't get it.

Fido does.

She didn't catch it, of course. She's not jumping yet. She waited till it came down, then fetched it. She didn't bring it to Lurena. She dragged it to me.

"That's my good girl!" I say, taking it from her. I scratch her mohawked head. She pants.

"Throw it again," Lurena says. "Only this time *to* me!"

I throw it, but lose my balance this time and fall over. The Frisbee shoots almost straight up, then slices back down, and lands high in a tree. And stays there.

"I guess Fido can't fetch *that* one!" Murph laughs.

"No, but look!" Lurena squeals. "Queen Girlisaur can!"

Fido's pup races up the tree trunk, then starts leaping from branch to branch.

"Oh, my stars!" Mom gasps.

When the pup reaches the Frisbee, she

nudges it with her nose till it drops from the tree and onto the grass.

Her mom zooms over and gathers it up.

"Thanks," I say after she brings it to me.

"Like mom, like daughter!" Lurena says, then laughs like it's the funniest thing anyone has ever said in the history of time.

My mom laughs, too, but no one else. It must be one of those things that's funny only to girls.

Fido sits at my feet, staring up at me, like she's waiting for something.

"What is it, girl?" I ask. "Do you want something?"

She gives a quick bark, then runs across the lawn to the garage. She scratches at the door.

"She wants something in the garage," Lurena says, brilliantly.

I know what it is. I'm the one who put it in there.

"Okay, Fido," I say. "I'll get it."

She stops scratching and starts barking happy barks.

Such a good dog.

Patrick Jennings

is the author of many popular novels for middle-schoolers, including *Guinea Dog, Lucky Cap, Invasion of the Dognappers, We Can't All Be Rattlesnakes,* and *Faith and the Electric Dogs.* He won the 2012–2013 Kansas William Allen White Children's Book Award and the 2011 Washington State Scandiuzzi Children's Book Award for *Guinea Dog,* which was also nominated for the following state lists: Massachusetts 2012–2013 Children's Book Award Master List, Colorado 2011–2012 Children's Book Award, New Hampshire 2011–2012 Great Stone Face Book Award, and Washington State 2014 Sasquatch Award. He lives in a small seaport town in Washington State.

You can visit him online at www.patrickjennings.com.